"Who writes the best romance fiction today?
No doubt it's Jayne Ann Krentz."
—*Affaire de Coeur*

The answer is repeated over and over again...

"Ms. Krentz has deservedly won the hearts of
readers everywhere with her unique blend of fiery
passion and romantic adventure.... One of the
great pleasures of reading Ms. Krentz is the
marvelous symmetry between characters and
plot.... It is this gratifying intricacy that makes
each and every Krentz book something to be
savored over and over again."
—*Rave Reviews*

"A master of the genre ... nobody does it better!"
—*Romantic Times*

"... Jayne Ann Krentz is a must for those who
enjoy romantic novels."
—*Brooklyn Record*

"The heroine sparkles, the chemistry sizzles, and
the hero leads the way—pure Krentz."
—*Romantic Times*
THE PRIVATE EYE
Harlequin Temptation

"A fun, witty romp...extremely entertaining...
quality of writing one expects from Ms. Krentz."
—*Rendezvous*
TOO WILD TO WED
Harlequin Temptation

"Wake up," Shannon murmured

Deliberately she trailed her fingertips through the curling hair on Garth's chest.

"Hey, that tickles," he complained with a small chuckle.

"What, this?" She traced a circle around one flat nipple. "Or this?" She drew her nails lightly down across his stomach. He clamped a hand over her roving palm, and excitement spiraled through her.

"Didn't your mother ever warn you about what happens when you tease a man?"

Shannon shivered. "My mother left most of my sex education to the schools. I don't recall them discussing teasing...."

Garth rolled over and sprawled on top of her, pinning her wrists above her head. "Then allow me to complete your education."

JAYNE ANN KRENTZ

THE TIES THAT BIND

Harlequin Books

TORONTO • NEW YORK • LONDON
AMSTERDAM • PARIS • SYDNEY • HAMBURG
STOCKHOLM • ATHENS • TOKYO • MILAN
MADRID • WARSAW • BUDAPEST • AUCKLAND

HARLEQUIN BOOKS

THE TIES THAT BIND
© 1986 by Jayne Ann Krentz

All rights reserved. Except for use in any review, the reproduction
or utilization of this work in whole or in part in any form by any
electronic, mechanical or other means, now known or hereafter
invented, including xerography, photocopying and recording, or in
any information storage or retrieval system, is forbidden without
the permission of the publisher, Harlequin Enterprises Limited,
225 Duncan Mill Road, Don Mills, Ontario, Canada M3B 3K9.

ISBN 0-373-83269-9

First Harlequin Books printing June 1986

Reprinted July 1993

All the characters in this book have no existence outside the
imagination of the author and have no relation whatsoever to
anyone bearing the same name or names. They are not even
distantly inspired by any individual known or unknown to the
author, and all incidents are pure invention.

® are Trademarks registered in the United States Patent and
Trademark Office and in other countries.

Printed in U.S.A.

1 C LASH

SHE HAD WATCHED HIM from her kitchen window for three mornings in a row. The routine varied little. He came out of the back door of the nearby cottage wearing a dark windbreaker, the collar pulled up against the chill of the early morning summer fog, and headed for the pebbly beach. There he disappeared into the mist, a stark, somber figure of a man enveloped by an eerie atmosphere that somehow suited him.

Shannon Raine stood at the window sipping her tea and wondered why she felt so oddly torn about introducing herself. It was a natural enough gesture to make. After all, he was a visitor here in this small community on California's rugged Mendocino coast. She was a permanent resident and his nearest neighbor. There would be nothing unusual or remarkable about simply following him down to the beach and wishing him a good morning.

Then again, a lot of visitors came and went during the summer around here, drawn by the spectacular coastal scenery, the quaint Victorian architecture of the tiny towns and the array of art galleries. Shannon reminded herself that she certainly didn't make an effort to introduce herself to all of the tourists who passed through the area.

But this man was different, and it wasn't simply because he happened to be staying in the immediate vicinity. Last summer the cottage had been filled with two vacationing mothers and their noisy brood of children. Shannon had had very little difficulty keeping her association with that crowd to a minimum. She was reasonably friendly by nature but not the sort who felt compelled to seek out others for companionship.

Perhaps it was the artist in her that made her content to spend long periods of time alone with a sketch pad or laboring over her silk screen. And perhaps that was what she sensed in the strange man who seemed so at home in the fog. He, too, was probably an artist. Shannon considered that possibility and then shook her head. No, it was far more likely the man was a writer or a poet. Yes, she could easily imagine him as a poet. There was a harsh, austere quality about him that told her he had discovered life to be a battle in many ways. Poets and other impassioned writers often found themselves at war with the world. Out of that inner conflict, Shannon supposed, sprang the fierce energy needed to put words together to form intense images. Idly she wondered how many restless, raging poets or writers drove silver-and-black Porsches like the one parked in front of her neighbor's cottage. The man must have had some measure of worldly success with his writing.

Shannon sipped her tea and reflected on the subject. Whatever his craft, she was certain of her analysis of the dark, brooding spirit that animated him. It touched a chord in her, and she couldn't ignore it. Only a man with a great capacity for passion would have to go through life with such a tight leash on himself.

With sudden decision Shannon set down her mug of tea and walked to the hall closet to pull out her plum-colored quilted jacket. It would be warm later on when the fog burned off and summer returned for a few hours, but this morning there was a distinct chill in the air.

The screen door slammed shut behind her as Shannon stepped out onto the back porch of her small, rustic cottage. For a moment she hesitated, inhaling the scent of the thick ocean air with absentminded pleasure. She had lived here for two years now, but she never ceased to enjoy the tangy smell of the sea. There was a raw, primeval richness to it that made her feel gloriously alive. Shoving her hands deep into the pockets of the jacket, she started down the short bluff to the beach. It was an easy descent in the daytime, and she didn't pause as the fog closed around her. Shannon knew where she was going. She had found her way down the short incline almost every day for two years. She thought she could probably do it in the dark now.

When she reached the rough beach she stopped, trying to decide in which direction her neighbor would have gone. The fog had reduced visibility to a matter of a few feet. The surf crashed a short distance away, sending lacy, curling tendrils to lap at her shoes. Shannon stepped back a few paces to avoid splashing her jeans. Then, on a whim, she turned to the left and started striding briskly along the water's edge.

She told herself she would handle this casually. After all, the beach was hers to use, too. She would be friendly and polite and see what happened at that point. Shannon was so busy deciding exactly how she would handle the introduction that she didn't even notice her quarry until he suddenly loomed up out of the fog. She nearly collided with him.

"Oh, excuse me, I'm sorry," she said quickly, feeling awkward now that the moment was upon her. This wasn't quite how she had planned the initial encounter. Hastily she recovered her balance and stood looking up at him. It was definitely a case of looking up. Shannon was a hairbreadth under five foot five, and as she lifted her eyes to his, she decided the stranger must have been close to six feet in height.

There was a certain sense of massiveness about him, although he was clearly built along lean, hard-edged lines. Her artistic eye automatically registered the overall impact of the dark, remote aloneness that seemed to radiate from him. The somber quality was reinforced physically by the near blackness of his hair, the ice-gray eyes and the roughly hewn angles of his face. Shannon did not find conventionally handsome men attractive. There was a shallow, uninteresting flatness about them that she had discovered was often accompanied by an equally shallow and uninteresting personality. The creative element in her instinctively responded to the more complex and the less easily defined, both in physical characteristics and in emotional makeup. At this moment everything in her was reacting with fierce awareness to the somber stranger.

"My name is Shannon Raine," she finally said when he made no reply to her awkward apology. "I'm your neighbor. Are you going to be staying long in the area?" She smiled, reaching up to push a curve of breeze-tossed hair out of her eyes.

"I'll be here for a while."

She nodded, accepting the ambiguity of his answer while she absorbed the deep, rough-textured sound of his voice. Its resonance made her want to reach for a sketch pad to see if she could find a visual representation of the dark textures. Already she could imagine an elaborately worked initial in the Carolingian style, classic and strong in overall proportion, but with intricate and complex details decorating the whole. The sort of image that compelled the viewer to keep studying it, every glance detecting a new element.

"I live here," she offered. When there was no immediate response, she added, "I walk down here most days. I hope you don't mind if I join you."

"Do I have any choice?"

She blinked, a little taken aback by the rudeness in spite of herself. "Well, I suppose I could go back to my place and wait until you're finished. Or we could walk in opposite directions."

He tilted his head slightly as if distantly amused by the touch of asperity in her voice. Then he shrugged and rammed his large hands back into the pockets of the windbreaker. "Suit yourself. I was just going to walk to the point and back."

"That's what I usually do." Shannon felt more confident now as she fell into step beside him. She had to move quickly in order to match his pace. He had a long, powerful stride, one that was curiously fluid in a purely masculine sense. She tried another smile on him, watching for some sign of response in his hard face.

There was no reaction to her smile as far as Shannon could tell, but after a long, thoughtful moment he said, "My name is Sheridan. Garth Sheridan."

Feeling as though she'd just gained a tremendous victory, Shannon nodded and launched into an innocuous discussion of the weather along the Mendocino coast in summer.

"We're famous for this fog, but the afternoons are usually quite pleasant. Most of us who live here like the fog, of course."

"Why?"

She was surprised by the flat question. She had always assumed the appeal of the fog was obvious. "Oh, I suppose because it's good for the artistic temperament," she said with a small laugh. "A lot of people who live around here are artists and writers."

"Which are you?"

"Sort of an artist," she admitted whimsically.

"Sort of an artist?"

"Some people might call me more of an illustrator. Or a designer. I design my own line of silk-screened greeting cards. I'm also experimenting with some silk-screen designs for tote bags and T-shirts. That sort of thing." She grinned suddenly and opened the front of her jacket to show him the coral-colored sweatshirt she was wearing underneath.

He stopped for a moment to stare down at the intricately worked design on the front of the shirt. It was a modern interpretation of the first character of an illuminated medieval manuscript. Shannon had chosen the letter *S* and embellished it with a wealth of fanciful flowers and birds. The colors were rich and strong, ranging from gold and red to an intense royal blue. Garth Sheridan studied the sweatshirt for a while and then asked blandly, "Is there much of a market for your work?"

Not everyone liked decorated sweatshirts, Shannon reminded herself as she closed the jacket. Still, for some reason she felt a vague disappointment. She had hoped he might like the design. It was one of her best. "Well, the greeting cards are starting to do all right, at least locally. A lot of shops in the area carry them, and the tourists seem to like them. I've only done a handful of the T-shirts and sweatshirts so far, but they sold out, so I'm hoping for a fairly good summer. I'm excited about my new line of tote bags. How about you?"

He resumed his ground-eating stride. "I haven't yet seen any of your tote bags."

Shannon pursed her lips. "I didn't mean that."

He hesitated. "I know." But there was no apology. He simply said, "I'm hoping for a fairly good summer, too."

She nodded. He was probably working on a book. "Are you going to spend the whole season here?"

"Unfortunately I can't do that."

"Ah," she said with a knowing smile. "Still trying to hold down a job while you wait for your big break?"

His mouth kicked up wryly at the corner. It was the first hint of a smile Shannon had yet seen, and it disappeared almost immediately.

"Yes. I'm still trying to hold down a job."

"It's tough trying to work a regular job and still find the time and energy you need for your art. I finally decided to take a chance a couple of years ago when my cards started selling on a fairly regular basis."

"What were you doing before you quit your job to become a card designer?"

Shannon's brows came together for an instant as she tried to determine whether there had been an underlying note of mockery in his question. Then she decided she was jumping to conclusions. "A little of this and a little of that. The usual things struggling artists and craftspeople do to make enough to pay the rent and buy supplies. I waited tables for a while, worked part-time in a library, did a stint in a department store—" She broke off and chuckled. "That didn't last long. I was only there for three days."

"What happened? Couldn't hack the regular hours?"

Now she was almost certain there was a hint of disapproval in his voice. "Not exactly. I flunked cash register training."

Garth's head came around abruptly. There was an incredulous expression on his face. "You what?"

Shannon waved one hand airily. "I flunked the training session that was supposed to teach the new employees how to handle the computerized cash registers. It was very humiliating. I mean, there I was with a college degree . . ."

"In fine arts, I presume."

"Uh, yes. At any rate, there I was surrounded by my fellow employees, many of whom hadn't gone any further than high school, and I just couldn't get the hang of handling all those little numbers. It's very complicated, you know. There are charge-card sales and refunds and exchanges and cash sales, not to mention inventory—control numbers and employee codes. And you have to be so precise. It must have been hard enough in the old days, but now with those computers all the big department stores have, it takes a mathematical genius to work as a salesclerk."

"A mathematical genius or a high school graduate," Garth said dryly.

Shannon sighed. "Yes, well, anyway, I flunked. But I managed to find work fairly routinely until I felt I was at a point where I could take the risk of going out on my own with the cards. It just takes perseverance. One of these days you'll reach the stage where you'll feel you can quit your regular job and devote yourself to what you really want to do."

"An interesting idea."

"Of course," she teased daringly, "you might have to sacrifice a few luxuries like the Porsche."

"I don't consider the Porsche a luxury."

"Oh." Before Shannon could think of a response, they arrived at the far end of the beach where a craggy point thrust out into the foaming water. The distant point was lost in the fog. Without a word Shannon and Garth halted and stood staring into the mist.

"You can't even tell where the land ends and the water begins," Garth finally observed.

"I know. It's the kind of scene where you half expect a ghost ship to suddenly appear out of the mist. An old-fashioned sailing ship, perhaps. One that's still flying the Jolly Roger."

"You have got an imagination, haven't you?" Garth turned and started back along the beach.

Shannon took a couple of extra quick paces to catch up with him. "Look, if you're not doing anything this evening, would you like to come over to my place for dinner? I'm having a couple of friends in, and you'd be quite welcome. Nothing fancy, I promise. Annie and Dan are very comfortable people."

"Annie and Dan?"

"Annie does macramé and Dan writes. He actually sold his first book this year. I'm sure you'd enjoy their company." Damn it, she wished she didn't sound quite so anxious. Shannon had intended the invitation to be supremely casual. Suddenly another thought occurred to her. "Perhaps you work in the evenings?"

"No. Not this evening."

"I see." She floundered, wondering what to say next. He wasn't accepting or declining the invitation. It made things awkward. Writers were often a little difficult, she reminded herself. One couldn't always expect normal manners from many of them. She had to make this as open-ended as possible. "Don't worry about making up your mind right away. I mean, there will be plenty of food, so if you decide to drop over at the last minute, feel free. Annie and Dan will be arriving around six."

"I'll keep it in mind."

So much for first contact, Shannon thought ruefully. If she had any sense, she would back off right now. It was clear the man was not the sociable type. A part of her wondered why she felt so compelled to draw him out. It was probably going to be a complete waste of time. Besides, she wasn't quite sure what she would do with Garth Sheridan if she succeeded in getting him to open up to her. She came to a halt on the beach and smiled with what she hoped was a casual charm.

"I guess I'd better get back to work. I have a lot of designing ahead of me today. I'm refining some sketches for the tote bags I told you about. See you around six, if you feel like dinner." Without waiting for a response she was certain wouldn't be forthcoming, anyway, Shannon nodded once and hurried up the short cliff.

At the top she turned to look down at him. Sheridan was standing on the beach, staring up at her. Even as she watched, a tendril of fog curled around him, partially veiling him from her sight. Shannon turned again and started toward her cottage. She had the oddest sensation of fleeing from something she didn't understand, and at the same time, she could feel the tug of invisible bonds urging her to go back and try again to break through the barriers surrounding Garth Sheridan.

Shannon was wise enough to recognize that some mysteries were better left alone. Unfortunately, perhaps, for her, she didn't think she was going to be able to leave Sheridan alone. Something in him was calling her, demanding further contact. She felt a little like a moth drawn to a shrouded flame.

By six o'clock that evening Shannon was convinced Garth Sheridan would not accept her invitation. With a curious sense of disappointment she finished setting the trestle table in front of the brick fireplace. The long runners that formed place mats had been screened in an exotic bird motif that she had designed three months ago during a long winter's weekend. She liked the birds with their otherworldly crests and flamboyant tail feathers and had idly considered using the design on a commercial batch of place mats.

She heard Dan Turcott's car crunching on the gravel in front of the cottage just as she was setting out the ceramic wine goblets that had been made by a friend in the town of Mendocino. Telling herself that she didn't really care if her reclusive neighbor failed to show, Shannon went to the door to greet her friends.

Annie O'Connor, her seven-months-pregnant figure outlined in a hand-embroidered jumper, reached the door first.

"Hi, Shannon, I'm starving," she said, grinning. Annie was the perfect image of an earth mother. There was a round fullness to her that, enhanced now by pregnancy, seemed to be the walking embodiment of the fertile female. She wore her long hair in braids, made her own clothes, her own bread and her own granola. She was close to Shannon's age, which was twenty-nine, but the two women bore little resemblance.

Instead of Annie's bosomy, motherly roundness, Shannon was slender with small, pert breasts and a graceful but not overly generous flare of thigh. She wore her seal-brown hair parted in the middle and falling in a casual curve that ended at the shoulder. The sweep of dark hair framed wide, heavily fringed hazel eyes and a soft mouth. There was a faint sprinkling of freckles across the assertive nose that lent a note of whimsy to Shannon's features. The whimsical motif was echoed in the snug-fitting jeans, the silkscreened sweatshirt and the well-broken-in leather loafers she wore.

"You've been starving for the past seven months." Dan laughed indulgently as he came around the hood of the old Volkswagen Bug he had lovingly maintained. He was a couple of years older than Annie, dark eyed and dark haired with a full mustache.

"You know how it is when you're eating for two," Annie said, patting her stomach complacently as she stepped through the door. "Umm. Smells delicious. What are we having, Shannon?"

"Pasta with olives and basil sauce and a salad. I got the basil fresh from Becky today. Don't worry, there's plenty."

Dan was smiling knowingly behind his mustache as he examined the fourth place setting at the table. "Expecting someone else?"

"Not any longer. If he were going to show I think he would have been here by now. He's a writer. Possibly a poet. You know the type, all dark and brooding and unpredictable. You can never tell what they'll do. I left the invitation open but I get the feeling he—"

The short double knock on the door she had just closed startled Shannon so much that she nearly jumped.

"Looks like your friend couldn't resist a free meal," Annie remarked.

"What starving writer could?" Dan asked philosophically as Shannon opened the door. He scanned the tall, dark figure on the threshold and added half under his breath to Annie, "This one looks like he needs his groceries on a regular basis."

Shannon ignored the comment as she smiled up at Garth. "I'm so glad you could come," she said, unaware of just how much welcoming warmth there was in her voice. She stood aside for him to enter and then hurriedly made introductions, which her visitors accepted politely.

"Sit down, all of you," Shannon requested, feeling remarkably happy as she hurried toward the kitchen with a new sense of anticipation. "I'll get the drinks. Annie, you're still on fruit juice?"

"Two more months of it and then I'll be free," Annie confirmed as Dan helped her gently into a chair.

Garth said nothing as he gravely took the goblet of Almaden Mountain White that Shannon offered. His crystal-colored eyes met hers for an instant, and she thought she saw a remote curiosity there. Whatever questions were going through his head, he didn't voice them. In fact, he didn't say much at all. He seemed content to sit in the overstuffed chair and drink his wine while he watched the other three with a distant gaze. It was only when Dan said something about his writing that Garth asked his first question.

"What sort of books do you write?"

"Those trashy glitz novels. You know the type. Everyone's sleeping with everyone else and all the characters are thoroughly neurotic." Dan grinned cheerfully.

"I don't read much fiction" was all Garth said. There was a moment of blank silence.

The conversation might have gone on the rocks then and there if it hadn't been for Annie. She started chatting determinedly about the crib she had located for the baby.

"Dan and I are going to refinish it next week. It's going to be lovely. Shannon, I was thinking of having you design some stencils I could use to decorate it. Interested? I could trade you a couple of macramé pot hangers."

"I'll be glad to do the stencils, but consider it a baby-shower gift. What would you like? Bunnies and teddy bears?"

"Are you kidding? I want some of those great illuminated letters you put on your greeting cards and totes. With any luck the kid will grow up learning how to read Medieval Latin."

"Not a very useful accomplishment," Garth observed.

There were a few seconds of awkwardness before Dan intervened to say, "Shannon tells me you're a writer, Garth."

Garth slanted a mildly reproving look at Shannon, who immediately got a sinking feeling in the pit of her stomach. "I wonder what made her think that?"

"Oh, Shannon has a rather vivid imagination," Dan said dryly. "I take it you're not a writer, then?"

"No. I run an electronics firm in San Jose."

Shannon nearly fell off her chair in astonishment. A businessman? Her dark, brooding poet? "I would never have guessed that."

"Then maybe your imagination isn't quite as vivid as your friends seem to think." Garth managed to soften the sarcasm but just barely. Before Shannon could think of a suitable response he was turning to Annie. "When is the baby due?"

Annie beamed, more than happy to discuss the impending event. "At the end of August. We're very excited." She transferred her smile to Dan, who grinned back briefly. "Fortunately Dan has just sold his first book, and the publishers seem quite anxious for another. Between the books and the macramé and some sewing work I'm going to be doing on Shannon's tote bags, I think we're going to be fine. Babies can be expensive, you know."

"So I've heard." Garth sipped his wine and then asked bluntly, "When are you two going to get married? If you're going to have a kid, Turcott, you owe it and its mother your name."

Shannon shot to her feet, every social instinct she possessed in full panic. "Dinner's almost ready. Annie, you and Dan go ahead and sit down while I get the salad out of the refrigerator. Annie, you sit on this side—it's more comfortable. Dan, you can have the bench near the fireplace. Why don't you put something on the stereo before you sit down? The Brandenburg Concertos would be nice, I think." With a determined expression she rounded on Garth. "You can give me a hand in the kitchen," she said very pointedly.

Garth hesitated. Then he obediently set down his goblet and followed Shannon into the kitchen. The joyous strains of one of the Bach concertos spilled out behind him as Shannon marched him into a corner and hissed, "Annie and Dan do not believe in marriage. They are a very devoted couple and are a good deal happier than many people I've known who are married. They are guests in my house, and I would appreciate it if you would kindly refrain from embarrassing them."

Garth said coolly, "If they don't believe in marriage, why does the subject embarrass them? I can understand why two adults would choose to live together instead of marrying. That's their business. But if your friend Dan is going to father a child, then he owes the kid and the mother the protection of his name."

"For heaven's sake! Don't you have any social tact at all? You just announced you were a businessman. Surely you've been obliged to learn some manners along the line. The business world has a few minimal requirements for social behavior."

The faintest trace of amusement came and went in his gaze as Garth asked softly, "Would I be exempt from such requirements as long as you thought I was a writer or a poet?"

"No. Even for a poet, you went too far in there. I just hope they can't hear us now." Shannon whirled and picked up a basket of sourdough bread. "Here. Make yourself useful. And try not to bring up the subject of marriage again."

Garth took the basket. "It shouldn't be hard. I'm not too fond of the subject myself." He walked back into the living room, leaving Shannon feeling intensely exasperated.

She had been so certain he possessed a deep, artistic soul. He had a lot of gall turning out to be a strait-laced businessman. From Silicon Valley, yet. It was incredible. Shaking her head over her own wayward imagination, Shannon went to the stove to finish the pasta preparations.

The rest of the evening passed in relative peace. Once Shannon was convinced Garth wasn't going to bring up any more socially unacceptable subjects she began to relax again. For their parts, Annie and Dan seemed quite at ease. The pasta with olives and basil vanished with satisfying rapidity.

It was somewhere toward the end of the meal that Shannon realized the revelations concerning Garth's occupation weren't having much effect on the strange compulsion she experienced around him. The remote aloneness she sensed in him still called to her, still made her deeply curious and still lured her close to the flame. Covertly she glanced at him from time to time, wondering at the watchful attitude he radiated.

"Any word yet on buyers for the tote bags and T-shirts?" Annie asked Shannon as she helped herself to another sourdough roll.

"No. I sent those samples off a month ago. I guess no one's interested."

"Well, it was just a shot in the dark," Dan consoled her. "You might have gotten lucky and interested some Bay area buyers, but the odds were against you. At least you know you've got a steady market around here. The same people who sell your cards will take the totes and shirts."

Garth frowned, looking at Shannon. "Did you just send your samples to the buyers unannounced? No preliminary contacts or follow-through?"

"I'm not a salesperson," Shannon retorted, sensing criticism. "If someone doesn't want my things, I'm not going to force them down his throat."

"If you can't do it properly, get someone else to market your products for you." Garth scooped out the last of the salad.

Shannon suppressed her irritated response for the sake of keeping peace at the table. "I'll think about it," she mumbled.

"You know, he might have a point," Dan said thoughtfully. "I know I'm going to look for an agent on this next book. The business side of things is hard for people like us."

"Do all artists and writers make such lame excuses for not paying attention to the business side of their work?" Garth asked.

Shannon took a deep breath and smiled brilliantly as she overrode the sarcastic question with one of her own. "Dessert, anyone? I've made strawberry short-cake."

"Sounds fantastic," Dan said.

"I'll give you a hand," Annie announced.

Shannon fled to the kitchen with her friend close behind. She could only hope that Garth would not start in on another lecture about the responsibilities of fatherhood in her absence. Oh, well. Dan could take care of himself. He was a quiet, competent sort of man. Soon the unfortunate dinner party would be over.

Annie and Dan took their leave an hour later. Shannon stood on the front step to see them off and wondered if Garth would depart now that the others had gone. As annoyed as she had been with him at various points in the evening, she suddenly realized she didn't want him to leave right away. As the Volkswagen disappeared into the evening fog, she closed the door and turned and smiled tentatively at the man sitting on the sofa covered in material she had silk-screened in a flower pattern. He was watching her with a curiously detached but expectant expression.

"Is that your Fiat parked outside?" he asked.

"Why, yes." She was startled at the unexpected question.

"Not much to it, is there?"

"I like it," she said with a shrug, again sensing disapproval but choosing to ignore it. "Would you, uh, like a glass of brandy before you leave?" She walked over to the old pine sideboard and picked up the brandy bottle and a glass.

"It depends. Is this the point in the evening where I'm supposed to seduce you?"

The shock of the coldly outrageous question caused Shannon to flinch. The glass in her hand fell to the floor with a shattering crash.

2

"I THINK YOU'D BETTER GO," Shannon said very quietly as she dropped to her knees to pick up the shards of glass. She kept her attention on her task so the embarrassed chagrin that must be in her eyes would not be so evident to Garth. "It's getting late, and I'm sure you've had enough socializing for the evening."

She heard him move from his seat on the sofa, but she didn't glance up. A few seconds later he crouched in front of her, reaching out to pick up some bits of the shattered glass. "Isn't that what this was all about?" Garth asked coldly.

"I don't know what you're talking about. Please, Garth, leave."

He put out a hand and tilted her chin so that she was forced to meet his eyes. The icy gaze was as remote as ever, but there was an element of assessment in it that disturbed Shannon more than she already was.

"I assumed part of my social obligations for the evening included making a pass," Garth said with breathtaking calm. "You pursued me rather persistently this morning. I got the feeling that you had the rest of the evening scheduled. It's all right, Shannon. I'll be happy to oblige."

"You can stuff your sense of obligation into the nearest trash can on your way out the door." Shannon jerked her chin out of his grasp and resumed picking up the remaining glass. "Good night, Garth."

He hesitated. "Look, Shannon, there's no need to play coy now. You certainly weren't acting that way earlier today. You were very up-front, in fact. It was refreshing, in a way."

"Please leave, Garth." Shannon got to her feet and carried the bits and pieces of glass into the kitchen. He followed, dumping the small shards he had picked up into the trash. There was nowhere else to retreat, so Shannon turned to face him, bracing herself against the sink. "You've made a few wrong assumptions, and I suppose it's my own fault. Don't worry, I won't mislead you any further."

He watched her broodingly. "If you want me to stay, Shannon, just say it. I prefer honesty. It's such a damn rare commodity."

Her initial shock and mortification gave way to a flash of temper. "I do not want you to stay," she bit out, each word emphasized as strongly as possible. "How's that for being up-front and honest? I want you out of my house immediately. You have completely misinterpreted my actions, and I don't feel like explaining them to you. Now get out."

He shrugged and turned to go. Shannon followed him to the front door, her eyes still reflecting anger and chagrin. Stiffly she held the door as he walked out onto the front steps. Garth turned once more to scan her face by the glow of the outside light. Then he nodded to himself and strode off toward his own cottage. In a moment he had disappeared into the evening fog.

Shannon slammed the door shut behind him, not caring if he heard the obvious manifestation of her temper, and slumped against the wood. Of all the stupid, embarrassing situations! What a fool she had made of herself. She should have abandoned the idea of getting to know him as soon as she'd discovered he wasn't really a writer or a poet or an artistic type of any kind. She couldn't imagine what had possessed her to ask Garth to stay late for a brandy.

Slowly she straightened away from the door, turned the old, worn-out lock and, with a groan of disgust, headed for the kitchen. It wasn't all her fault, she told herself bracingly. After all, Garth hadn't exactly been forthcoming about either his occupation or his assumptions. And he'd had the nerve to accept her invitation to dinner, during which he'd managed to drop more than one clangor into the conversation. His behavior was inexcusable. She would not berate herself further. Somewhat defiantly she helped herself to a shot of the brandy she had attempted to serve earlier to her guest.

Outside in the fog, Garth paused on the top step of his cottage and glanced back at Shannon's house while he dug his key out of his pocket. The heavy mist turned her front door light into a ghostly glow, and the bulk of her cottage was an unreal shadow. For a jarring moment his mind played with an unsettling fantasy of a fairy lady living in a gossamer castle.

He had been invited to dinner in the castle and had blundered badly. Garth shoved the key in the lock and sighed deeply. Odds were he wouldn't get a second invitation.

With a nagging sense of regret he closed the door and walked into the tiny kitchen alcove to find the bottle of whiskey he had brought with him from San Jose. He poured himself a generous shot and carried the glass out into the living room. There he sprawled in an old, slipcovered chair that probably dated from the forties. It brought to mind the fact that in a couple more years he, too, was going to hit forty. He wondered if by then he would need reupholstering as badly as the chair did. There was no doubt he was beginning to feel the wear and tear of his life.

Leaning his head back against the cushion, Garth closed his eyes and savored the bite of the whiskey. It would have been much more pleasant, he admitted to himself, to be sipping brandy with the lady in the castle next door. A picture of a handful of freckles scattered beneath intelligent, inquiring eyes popped into his head. There was more than intelligence and inquiry in that wide, feminine gaze. There was a hint of promise, too.

He didn't have to analyze his own actions to know why he'd behaved the way he had this evening. The reason was simple enough. He'd wanted to shatter the illusion before someone else did it for him.

From the moment Shannon had tumbled out of the fog this morning, nearly colliding with him, he had been wary. There was nothing unusual about that. It was Garth Sheridan's nature to be cautious with others. He had known too many people who couldn't be trusted. Normally he had no trouble keeping others at a distance.

But something was different in this case. Something was substantially different when it came to dealing with Shannon Raine. He hadn't planned to accept her dinner invitation because he hadn't been able to figure her out. He would have preferred to have her fully analyzed, assessed and understood before getting involved with her. Yet when six o'clock had arrived this evening he had found himself locking his door and walking the short distance between his cottage and the fairy castle.

Garth had had women pursue him before, but usually because they had learned he was a financially successful male who happened to be unattached and not terribly ugly. He was fairly certain it wasn't his innate charm that had drawn them. Charm was not his long suit. Men who were by nature loners and by experience accustomed to betrayal never developed charming personalities.

He considered that and winced. Even by his own standards he had been a particularly uncharming dinner guest this evening. Now as he sat drinking whiskey alone, it occurred to him that he'd probably destroyed a rather special and delicate bud without

ever giving it a chance to flower, simply because he
didn't trust flowers in general. Chances were Shannon would never give him a second opportunity to get
to know her. He had seen the stunned embarrassment in her hazel eyes tonight and he'd seen something else there, too, something that he could have
sworn was a degree of pain.

SHANNON HAD WALKED into town to collect her mail
the next morning without any sense of anticipation.
Therefore, the letter on buff-colored paper with its
distinctive return address took her by complete surprise. She tore it open on the post office steps and
scanned the contents with mounting excitement.
Then, feeling enormously more lighthearted than she
had ten minutes earlier, she decided to treat herself to
a cup of tea at the small café across the street. Maybe
one of her friends would be there. She wanted to tell
someone the good news.

The café was busy with a healthy-sized morning
crowd, but everyone she saw seemed to be a tourist.
A little disappointed, she took a stool at the counter
and ordered her tea, then read the letter a second time.
She was poring over the contents when Garth Sheridan straddled the stool beside her.

"Good news?" he asked calmly, signaling the waitress for coffee.

Shannon frowned for an instant and then relaxed.
She was too elated to be angry at anyone this morning, even Garth. "A buyer for a San Francisco bou-

tique says she wants to visit me in a couple of weeks
to talk about my new line of tote bags. She says she
loves the sample I sent and wants to discuss production and shipping schedules. She isn't from one of the
big chains, but this shop is a very elegant one off
Union Square. It would be a wonderful outlet for the
bags. Very classy."

"Congratulations. What *are* your production and
shipping schedules?"

Shannon flushed, some of her elation fading. "I'm
not sure. Do you think she'll be expecting a minifac-
tory in my home? I wonder how many bags a week
she'll want. It takes time to hand-screen the fabric and
then it has to be stitched together. Annie is going to
help me with the sewing, but we haven't really dis-
cussed how many she could do a week. She has to
have time for her macramé work, after all. I can't expect her to devote all her time to the bags. Of course,
this buyer may not want too many at first—" Shannon broke off, nervously tapping the buyer's letter on
the countertop as she considered all the problems
ahead.

"If you want to impress the buyer you'd better have
the logistics worked out before she arrives. You'll want
her to think you're in complete control of the business end of things. Otherwise she'll probably think she
can take advantage of you. And if she thinks that, she
will." Garth stirred his coffee.

"Take advantage of me? Why should she do that?
Are you always so cynical, Garth?"

"Usually. I've been in the business world a long time."

"Don't remind me." Shannon's voice was laced with remembered chagrin.

There was a pause and then Garth said carefully, "I'm sorry I gave you the wrong impression about my, uh, occupation. I suppose in your world businessmen aren't exactly at the top of the social heap."

"Especially when they accept dinner invitations and then proceed to insult the hostess and her guests," Shannon retorted with spirit.

He had the grace to wince. "If I'd been a surly brooding poet, would you find it easier to forgive me?"

Startled, Shannon eyed him with a skeptical gaze. "Is this some sort of apology?"

"Yes."

"Why?"

He met her eyes. "Now who's being cynical?"

"After last night, I'm inclined to be cautious."

A faint smile edged his mouth. "I doubt if you know the meaning of the word."

"What's that supposed to mean?" she challenged as the waitress slapped the check on the counter. Before she could grab the slip of paper, Garth reached out and picked it up.

"Never mind. I'll buy this morning. I owe you something for the excellent dinner last night. I don't think I even remembered to thank you for it."

"No, you didn't."

"Finished? We can walk back to the cottages together."

Shannon struggled for an excuse and came up with what seemed a reasonable one. "I was going to pick up some groceries first."

Garth nodded. "Not a bad idea. I'll need some things for dinner, too."

Shannon sighed to herself and accepted the inevitable. Short of staging a small scene, there was no smooth way to avoid him. Grudgingly, she left the counter and waited while he paid the tab. He followed her out onto the sidewalk, and together they turned toward the grocery store at the far end of the town's single business street.

"The fog has almost cleared off," Garth noted politely. "Should be a nice, warm afternoon."

"Probably." Shannon was embarrassed by her short response, but she was determined not to add anything else. Let Garth try to force the conversation for a change.

"You like living here." It was an observation, not a question.

"I love it."

"Are all your friends artsy-craftsy types?"

She glared up at him. "If you mean are most of them artistically and creatively oriented, yes. If you don't care for the breed you shouldn't have rented a cottage along the Mendocino coast. Everyone knows this is a haven for writers and artists and craftspeople."

"I didn't come here for the people."

Shannon thought about that for a moment. "No, I don't suppose you did. You surprise me, you know. I thought business types were fairly social by nature. You know, slick-talking salesmen, smooth-tongued corporate executives and so on. I would have thought you'd prefer a vacation spot that featured a couple of golf courses, maybe a tennis court and a few gourmet restaurants. Someplace where the rest of your kind hang out."

"Just because I make my living in the business world it doesn't mean I've completely adapted to the lifestyle," Garth said quietly.

Shannon, who had been anticipating a more cutting response, again experienced a shaft of embarrassment. "I'm sorry. I shouldn't have made nasty remarks." She came to a halt. "Here's the grocery store. I won't be more than a few minutes."

"Take your time," he began to say and then realized she had already darted inside.

Shannon said hello to the clerk behind the checkout counter and then wheeled an old, crotchety cart toward the vegetable section at the rear of the store. She was acutely aware of Garth heading down the frozen-food aisle. This really was an awkward situation, she decided. The last thing she had expected from him was an apology, and she wasn't at all sure how to interpret it. She knew that in spite of her resolve to ignore him, she was weakening under his new, polite approach.

Perhaps Garth Sheridan was simply regretting the fact that he'd wrecked his chances for a short vacation affair and was trying to recover lost ground. If so, he had a surprise coming. She wasn't going to weaken that much. She was not setting herself up for any such affair. She would remain cool and polite and distant now that she knew the situation for what it was.

But in spite of her good intentions she couldn't resist frowning at Garth as he came around the corner of the aisle carrying a couple of cans of vegetables and two frozen entrées. Shannon spoke before she stopped to think.

"Why on earth do you want to buy canned vegies when there's nice fresh broccoli and some excellent tomatoes in the vegetable bins over there?" She waved in the general direction of the fresh vegetable section.

"It's easier to open a can."

She shook her head. "It's just as easy to cook fresh broccoli."

"Maybe it's easier for you, but not for me. I've never cooked fresh broccoli."

"Put those cans back on the shelf and I'll show you how to cook your own vegetables," Shannon said before she could change her mind. She held her breath, calling herself every kind of fool. Then, without a word, Garth replaced the canned vegetables and went to pick up a bunch of fresh broccoli.

"It's a deal," he said softly.

She was an idiot. That was the only explanation. A complete and utter idiot. Shannon berated herself while she stood with Garth in the checkout line. She asked herself what on earth she thought she was doing as they walked together back toward the cottages, and she decided she was probably nuts to be thinking of inviting Garth over for dinner again that night so that she could show him how to cook broccoli.

"Will there be anyone else coming?" he asked when she extended the invitation on the way back to the cottages.

"No," she responded.

He nodded. "Good. I don't enjoy social situations. I'll see you around six."

Shannon stared after him as he turned and headed toward his own cottage. She wondered what she represented to him if he didn't see her as a "social situation."

TWO DAYS LATER Shannon no longer worried how Garth viewed their relationship. Since the night of the broccoli-cooking exhibition everything between herself and Garth had somehow shifted into a new and gently rewarding course. She was aware of a bubbling sense of happiness and anticipation whenever she saw him or thought of him. It was at the back of her mind when she worked on her sketches, and it was there during the hours she spent drawing the blade of the squeegee down the silk-screen frame to produce her greeting cards.

Garth's attitude was becoming increasingly indulgent and familiar, but he had studiously avoided any overtly sensual approaches. It was as if he sensed he had nearly ruined things that first evening and was determined not to repeat his mistake.

On the afternoon of the second day, Shannon sat cutting out a stencil of a letter *A* that she had designed in a medieval Anglo-Saxon style. The *A* was a frame for a hunting scene with fanciful creatures playing along the legs of the letter.

As she worked she pondered the fact that she was soon going to be ready for Garth to repeat his "error" of the first night. She wouldn't mind now at all if he showed some interest in making a pass. The thought made her smile as she used the fine, sharp blade of her knife the way she would a pencil to cut out the portions of the design that would be printed in red. The canvas fabric she intended to silk-screen the next day would have to be run through the screening process a different time for each color used. She would start with the red. When she had finished with that batch she would let the ink dry and then run the fabric sections through again to apply the yellow portion of the design. The process would continue until she had completed the illustration on each canvas square. Then the fabric would be sewn into tote bags. She wanted some especially good examples of her work for the buyer who was due to pay her a visit.

It occurred to Shannon that she might have to find a subtle way of letting Garth know she was no longer adverse to the idea of taking their relationship to a more intimate level. He was being so cautious that it was almost humorous.

Shannon finished cutting the film and set the knife down on her worktable. Critically she examined her creation and was satisfied with the sharp, crisp lines. It should print well. Tomorrow she would attach it to the frame and run off a few samples. Laying the film down on the table, she leaned forward on her elbows and studied the cottage across the way.

The afternoon sun was warm, and the day was balmy with a pleasant breeze off the sea. There was no sign of Garth, however. He didn't seem to be making any effort to enjoy the fine day. He rarely appeared in the afternoons, Shannon realized. She was beginning to wonder how he spent his time inside the cottage. It hadn't seemed polite to ask.

Idly she glanced at the calendar on the wall and saw that she had circled today's date in red. In tiny letters she had noted "T of S at 8. Must go Verna prod." Hastily Shannon deciphered the cryptic reminder and came to a sudden decision. Hopping down off the drafting chair, she left the cottage and went to knock on Garth's front door.

There was a short delay before Garth appeared at the door. He looked at her bemusedly for a moment, as if he had been in another world when she'd knocked. His shirt was open, the sleeves were rolled up on his forearms and he was barefoot. His dark hair was in disarray, as if he had been running his fingers through it. All in all, he appeared to have been very much involved in something when she had knocked. His expression cleared abruptly as he realized who stood on the threshold. Shannon was certain that he was pleased to see her. She wished his eyes would soften a bit more often the way they did now. He had terrific eyes.

"I just came over to see if you'd like to go with me to a local theater production tonight," Shannon began lightly, glancing curiously around the room. There was a pile of business documents and papers spread out on the old table in the corner. "A friend of mine is producing and directing it, and it should be interesting. They're doing *The Taming of the Shrew* and I can't wait to see how Verna has interpreted it. She's a strong feminist with very radical feelings on the subject of women's roles. I can't imagine how she'll handle Kate and Petruchio." Shannon plowed to a halt, her curiosity getting the better of her. "Uh, are you working?"

"I was."

"On your vacation?"

Garth shrugged. "Why not?"

"Why not? Well, because you're supposed to be on vacation. What's the point of taking time off if you keep on working?"

"This is something that has to be done, Shannon. It's a crucial bid proposal my company will be submitting in a few weeks."

"Is that right?" She wandered over to the table and glanced down at the array of papers. "Good grief! They're all stamped Confidential." She backed away from the table and threw him an uncertain glance. "I guess I shouldn't be looking at them."

"They're company confidential, not government confidential." He came forward and shuffled the papers into a neat stack. "I don't think it much matters if you look at them. You've said yourself you flunked your cash register training course and business, in general, doesn't seem to be your forte. I doubt you'd find much of interest in these." He gave her a look of indulgent amusement.

"Let's not be patronizing," Shannon murmured sardonically. "Maybe I'm a corporate spy in disguise, sent here to arrange a so-called accidental meeting with you and then steal your bid proposal."

To her surprise he didn't seem to find the comment amusing. "No," Garth said evenly, "I don't think you're the company spy type."

"Have you known many?" she demanded, mildly resentful of his certainty. She was pretty sure it stemmed from his condescending attitude toward her lack of business acumen. Besides, no woman enjoys being told she lacks some aura of mystery, Shannon decided.

"I've known a few. The high-tech firms in Silicon Valley are always fighting a constant battle against corporate as well as international espionage. In my line of work spies of all kinds are a constant hazard.

Almost as common as back-stabbing co-workers and hustling corporate-ladder climbers."

Shannon was appalled, not so much by the words but by his grim acceptance of his own world. "It sounds a little rough."

"You get used to it."

"Used to back-stabbing co-workers, hustling ladder climbers and spies? How could anyone get used to that?"

Garth smiled abruptly, startling her. Then, with lazy gentleness, he put out his hand and touched the curving sweep of her dark hair. "A man can become accustomed to a lot more than that, Shannon. He can also get used to the idea of not being able to trust anyone, especially a woman."

She went very still. "Are you like that? Unable to trust anyone at all?"

He let that pass. "What time is the play?"

"What? Oh, eight o'clock. Are you interested?"

"Definitely." His expression said he meant it. "I'll come over and pick you up around seven-thirty. Will that give us enough time?"

Shannon nodded, glad that he seemed to want to be with her but uneasy over the way he had switched the subject just as they were getting to a very important issue. If Garth didn't trust anyone, especially women, how did he really feel about her? She needed to know, Shannon thought as she said goodbye and left him to his bid work. She needed to know he trusted her, that she was the exception in his life.

It was only when she reached her own cottage that she asked herself just why it was so important that she be the exception. The answer wasn't one she wanted to deal with just then. Everything was too new, too uncertain between herself and Garth Sheridan.

But sooner or later she had to have all the answers about this man. The compulsion to know him completely was stronger than ever.

WHEN THE DOOR CLOSED behind Shannon, Garth moved to the window to watch her walk back to her cottage. For a long time after she had disappeared inside the other house, he stood lost in thought.

Something about Shannon reminded him of how it had all been back at the beginning of his career. Back before the reality of his world had set in and he had forced himself to face that reality. She was honest, enthusiastic, happy with the life she had created for herself. There was a gentle freshness about her that he found himself wanting to shield and protect. He hoped she never woke up to the same reality he had awakened to find. Any man with whom she got involved would have an obligation to keep her safe and untainted by the hard side of life. But how many men could be trusted to fulfill that obligation, he wondered. Certainly none that he knew.

Then he grinned ruefully at his own false altruism. He wanted to do more than protect Shannon from the real world—he wanted to keep her safe for himself, and he was honest enough to admit it. There was something in Shannon that he suddenly realized he wanted and needed. Something he hadn't touched or held in a long, long while. Perhaps he'd never really possessed what Shannon offered. The deep hunger that flared in him was unsettling. He made himself turn back to the pile of papers on the table.

THE THEATER HAD ONCE been a barn and the gray, weathered timber frame had been retained for atmosphere. A stage had been constructed in the center. Verna Montana's production of *The Taming of the Shrew* was done in the round. Garth and Shannon had excellent seats.

"What's the matter? Couldn't the actors afford costumes?" Garth muttered as the play opened. "I know small-town theater troupes are usually hard up for cash, but they could have at least come up with a few fake daggers and long skirts."

"Verna wanted to try something different, so she decided to do the play in modern dress. Now hush," Shannon whispered as the show began.

It was soon apparent that Verna's theatrical vision had been paired with her feminist ideology to create a radically new version of Shakespeare's play. Kate, of course, had always been a strong character in the original, but under Verna's direction she became a modern, politically astute feminist. Shannon watched in astonishment as she somehow managed to make Petruchio appear to be the manipulated one in the story. Flamboyant, strident and infinitely smarter than the man who was supposed to master her, Verna's Kate dominated the play. Every scene in which she was supposed to be tamed somehow became a scene in which Petruchio appeared to be subtly led around by a ring in his nose. While he assumed he was mastering his wife, she was finding him amusing and childishly simple to handle.

Kate laughed at him, scolded him, pretended to be in awe of him and eventually had him in the palm of her hand. When, at the end of the play, Petruchio bragged about Kate's wifely accomplishments, it was clearly a case of a man whose ego was so bloated that it wouldn't allow him to see that it was his wife who now ran the house and him.

There was a thunderous round of applause and a good deal of laughter as the play came to a close, and Shannon turned to grin at Garth.

"You've got to admit, Verna gave the play a distinctive touch."

"She ruined it." Garth took Shannon's arm and guided her out into the damp night. His Porsche stood amid the motley assortment of vehicles in the dusty parking lot.

"Nonsense. It was a very witty interpretation," Shannon argued. "What do you say we go have some ice cream and discuss the matter like reasonable people?"

"Ice cream?"

"There's an ice-cream shop across the street from the grocery store. On play nights it stays open late to catch the after-theater crowd."

"One would never have guessed you were so cosmopolitan out here in the sticks," Garth remarked dryly as he slid the sleek car out onto the road behind a row of other vehicles. "Okay, ice cream it is. But I'm not sure we'll be able to discuss the play in a reasonable fashion. There was nothing reasonable about that production. Shakespeare is probably turning over in his grave."

"Verna did a fascinating job of updating the characters! There, you can park in front of the grocery store. I see a space."

Garth obediently pulled the Porsche into the slot and followed Shannon into the ice-cream parlor, where a number of other people were gathering to eat chocolate sundaes and analyze Verna Montana's unique version of *The Taming of the Shrew*. It was a good-natured crowd of laid-back people who took great pleasure in their small-town life-style and their artistic endeavors. Several people greeted Shannon as she walked into the room. She responded with a cheerful wave and zeroed in on a small vacant table near the center of the busy parlor.

"I'll hold the table and chairs. You go get the orders," she told Garth. "I'll have a double scoop of vanilla ice cream, double fudge sauce, nuts and double whipped cream."

"You have a hearty appetite, woman. I can see you're going to be expensive to feed." He left her to stand in the line of ice-cream purchasers.

Shannon grinned as she watched him standing there and wondered how long it had been since Garth had waited in line to order ice-cream sundaes. He glanced across the room, saw the laughter in her eyes and grinned back. The slashing expression of amusement had a pirate's ruthlessness behind it, but it was a genuine smile. It was one of the few times that she had seen real laughter in his face. Shannon faced the fact that she loved seeing him smile. Every time she coaxed one out of him she felt as if she had uncovered buried treasure.

He returned to the table a few minutes later carefully balancing two magnificent fudge sundaes. The room was alive with the spirited voices of people arguing about the play.

"Now about the abomination we just witnessed," Garth began as he dug into his ice cream. "Your friend Verna has a lot to answer for. I'll admit I haven't seen *The Taming of the Shrew* in several years, but I do remember Petruchio didn't come off looking like a clown."

"He does in Verna's production," Shannon declared triumphantly. "And about time, too. The way Kate handles Petruchio in this version, it's clear that she was the one in charge right from the beginning. I don't know why I haven't ever seen that potential in the play."

"You haven't seen it in the play because Shakespeare never put it in to begin with," Garth argued. "Kate is supposed to be spirited, but she's not supposed to be a conniving manipulator."

Shannon leaned forward aggressively and aimed her long ice-cream spoon accusingly at Garth. "Verna made several excellent points tonight, not the least of which is that men usually don't even know when they're being manipulated by a woman. Their egos are usually so inflated they assume they're always the one in charge."

"Shannon, you don't know what you're talking about."

"Ha!" Her chin lifted defiantly, her eyes sparkling with the light of battle. "If a smart woman like Kate plays her cards right, she can manipulate her Petruchio for the rest of his life and he'll never even know what happened."

"I promise you I wouldn't be that stupid."

"That's what they all say," Shannon informed him jubilantly. The ice-cream spoon moved in an arc to indicate the entire world of males.

"Shannon . . ."

"I'll bet every man alive secretly thinks he's the dominant partner in a relationship. I don't care how liberated he is, his ego is still functioning in the Dark Ages. That's another point Verna made beautifully tonight."

"Shannon, you're getting carried away." Garth eyed the waving ice-cream spoon.

"Verna's production brings home the fact that men haven't really changed much since Shakespeare's time. Putting the characters in modern dress emphasizes that, don't you think? It was a brilliant idea."

"I think," Garth said carefully, "that you'd better quiet down and eat your ice cream before you get us thrown out of here."

"They don't have bouncers in ice-cream parlors," she told him loftily. "Now, another point Verna made tonight was one about Petruchio's real reason for marriage. He was a mercenary, greedy man who got what he deserved. As far as I'm concerned, he—"

"Shannon."

"He had it coming. What's more, thanks to Verna's version of the story, I now see that the character of Kate represents all the basic female strengths. She—"

Shannon got no further. Garth surged to his feet, planted two large hands on her shoulders, leaned down and kissed her heavily on the mouth. The flow of fiery argument was sealed forever in Shannon's throat. She was as startled by the leashed hunger in the kiss as she was by the outrageous action itself. In that moment everything changed between them. An invisible barrier had been crossed, and nothing would ever be quite the same. Her eyes opened wide in silent, stunned astonishment.

There was a wave of laughter and applause from the other patrons of the ice-cream parlor as Garth slowly lifted his head and stood looking into Shannon's wide hazel eyes.

"Attaboy, Petruchio," someone yelled good-naturedly from across the room. "Show her who's boss."

Shannon didn't move as Garth sat down again and picked up his spoon.

"Eat your ice cream, Shannon," Garth advised gently.

Without a word Shannon stabbed her spoon back into the fudge sundae.

3

THE SHORT DRIVE BACK to the cottages from the ice-cream parlor was made in absolute silence. For the first time since she had met Garth, Shannon couldn't think of anything to say. It was an odd sensation, as if something very delicate and fragile was taking shape and she dared not shatter it before it had completely formed. She was grateful for the damp, foggy darkness that shielded her face as Garth parked the car in front of his cottage, got out and opened her door.

Shannon realized she was holding her breath as he led her around the hood of the Porsche. She started breathing again when Garth guided her past his own front door and across the short distance to hers. She didn't know whether to feel relieved or disappointed. What she actually felt was a little light-headed. They came to a halt on her front step, and Garth fitted her key into the lock. When the door swung open he looked down at her, studying her face in the dim front-door light. His hand lifted to touch her hair, and then he raised his other hand and wrapped his fingers warmly around the nape of her neck, cradling her head as he lowered his mouth to hers.

Shannon murmured something soft and unde-fined, but the faint words were sealed behind her lips as she felt once again the heavy, leashed hunger in him. She had not imagined it earlier this evening when he had taken her by surprise in the ice-cream parlor. There was a driving desire burning deep inside this man, and tonight she was the focus of it.

"Shannon, please invite me in." He spoke against her mouth.

"For brandy?" Her voice was a tremulous whisper. She was vividly aware of the warmth of his fingers on her skin.

"No, not for brandy. For bed."

He found her mouth again with his own and under the persuasive, relentless pressure, Shannon's lips parted. Garth groaned thickly as he deepened the kiss. His hands slid slowly down Shannon's back, urging her more closely against him. Shannon wasn't even aware of the way she had already slipped her arms around his neck. She could feel the warmth and the strength in him and nothing had ever felt so right.

"Shannon?"

He wasn't coming inside the cottage without an invitation tonight, she realized. It would be simple enough to refuse him. He wouldn't fight her decision. Perhaps it was symbolic. She had been the one to issue all the invitations so far in this relationship. Perhaps Garth wanted her to issue this one, too. The knowledge should have given her a small sense of feminine power. It might have if Shannon hadn't been so deeply aware of her own desire and need. She tilted her head back against his arm and looked up at him.

"I wouldn't want you to feel under any sense of, uh, social obligation," she said.

"Don't tease me, Shannon. Not tonight. Even if I deserve it." His voice was husky. "Just tell me I can come inside and make love to you."

She leaned her head against his shoulder. "Come inside and make love to me, Garth," she whispered.

His arms tightened around her, and she felt the relief and masculine anticipation leaping through him. Then Garth was leading her inside the cottage, closing the front door and locking it. She heard him play with the loose lock for a moment.

"This thing must have been installed forty years ago. You should get something more secure put in."

Shannon felt a kind of gentle amusement at the thought that he could notice something as mundane as her door lock after having kissed her with such passion. "I'll think about it," she promised softly, instantly forgetting the whole matter as he pulled her closer.

Garth didn't reach out to turn on the hall light. In the darkness he kissed her again, his mouth heavy and warm and lingering.

"I've wanted you since that first day but I made such a mess of things that night after your dinner party. I've regretted it ever since."

She silenced him by standing on her tiptoes and brushing a feather-light kiss against his lips. "It's all right, Garth."

"I want to explain."

"Later. You don't have to explain now."

He shuddered heavily, gathering her into his arms. "I'll make this good, sweetheart. I promise."

Her mouth curved faintly in a soft smile. "I told you, I don't want you to feel any sense of social obligation."

"You're a tease," he growled, pushing aside a sweep of dark hair to kiss the delicate place behind her ear. "I wonder why I didn't realize that before."

"You're still getting to know me."

"True. But by tomorrow morning, I'll know most of your secrets."

"Will you?"

"I'll make it a priority. You're trembling," he observed, running his palms down to her hips and back up to her shoulder. "Are you nervous, honey?"

"Yes," she said honestly.

"Don't be," he ordered softly. "This is right. I can feel it."

"I know." She was as certain of it as he seemed to be.

Garth brought his mouth back down on hers, lifted her into his arms and started down the short hall. When he came to a halt beside the first door, Shannon shook her head against his shoulder.

"No," she whispered. "Not that one. That's my studio. The next one."

He tightened his grip on her and walked through the next door into her bedroom. Shannon's bed stood waiting in the shadows, its silk-screened quilt and huge pillows beckoning invitingly. Garth stood Shannon on her feet and smiled down at her. In the darkness she could see the desire that was flaring in his eyes and the sensual tension that edged his smile.

"When you look at me like that," he said, "I feel as if I'll come apart if I don't get you into bed."

She leaned against him, aware of a melting feeling that made it difficult for her to stand. "I didn't know," she managed.

"Until I kissed you tonight in the ice-cream parlor?"

She nodded. "I didn't realize until then that you wanted me."

"I want you, Shannon," he told her softly. His fingers went to the buttons of the turquoise silk blouse she wore with her jeans that evening. Deliberately he slipped each one open until the garment came completely undone.

Slowly Garth pushed the silk from her shoulders, his fingers sliding up under the hem of the camisole she had put on underneath the blouse. Shannon felt his thumbs gliding over the tips of her breasts as the undergarment was lifted over her head. Then she was naked to the waist and achingly conscious of his pleasure in her nudity. Garth cupped one small, gently rounded breast in his hand.

"So soft and delicate," he said wonderingly. "And so sleek and sexy."

Shannon gave a husky, nervous little laugh and pressed herself against him, burying her face in his shirt. "I'm very glad you're not hung up on the *Playboy* centerfold type."

"I'm hung up on the real and genuine type. The honest type. There aren't many of them around. But you're one of them, aren't you, Shannon?"

She lifted her head, sensing the dark shades of meaning behind the words but uncertain of exactly what he was trying to say. It was important that she understand, she realized. Somewhere in his comment lay a key she needed to fully comprehend this man. There was so much she didn't know about him yet.

But tonight was not a night for asking questions. The passionate urgency flowing between herself and Garth was the dominant force at the moment. He wanted her and she knew, even though she hadn't realized it at first, that she wanted him. Instead of trying to answer his odd question, she lifted her palms to his shoulders and turned her lips to the strong column of his throat.

"Ah, Shannon, you're so sweet. My God, how did I go this long without you?" Garth tugged at the fastening of her jeans, sliding them down over her hips and drawing the lacy scrap of her panties off with the denim. When she stepped free of the last of her clothing he clenched his fingers into the flare of her buttocks and groaned as he pulled her close.

For a long moment he seemed content to hold her like that, but when she stirred restlessly against him Garth laughed shakily and set her free. Then he tugged down the quilt. Shannon slipped between the sheets, her eyes never leaving Garth as he stripped off his own garments.

His body was hard with his desire, sending a primitive thrill through Shannon. In the shadows the utter maleness of him was both intimidating and enthralling. The strong planes of his chest and shoulders tapered to a flat stomach and muscular thighs. When Garth slid into bed beside her, reaching for her, Shannon was fiercely glad that she was capable of making him want her to this extent. She could feel the need in him and longed only to satisfy it.

"Garth, I want you," she whispered, wondering at the intensity of her own desire. "I didn't realize until now. I didn't understand why I had to keep trying to get to know you. It's never been like this with any other man."

He leaned over her, kissing the hollow of her throat while·his hands began exploring her body. "By tomorrow morning you'll know me as well as I'll know you. I swear it."

Garth wanted to reassure her even more, but right now he couldn't find any other words except the ones he needed to tell her how sweet and hot and sensual she was. All his instincts were clamoring for him to slake the sudden thirst that was driving him. It had been building during the past few days, simmering deep inside him without his fully realizing the extent of it. But this evening when, on impulse, he'd silenced her with a kiss, Garth had nearly been swamped with his own need. If they hadn't been sit-

ting in an ice-cream parlor full of laughing playgoers
he would have pulled Shannon down on the floor and
made love to her then.

But now she was here, lying beneath him, opening
herself fully and completely. Garth was fascinated
with the honesty of Shannon's own reactions. He
drew his palm over her small breast and felt the nipple flower at his touch. Her fingers trailed through his
hair and then sank into his shoulders when he touched
the silky skin of her inner thigh. Her responsiveness
nearly drove him out of his mind.

"That's it, honey," he breathed as she lifted herself
against his hand. "Come to me, let me have you. I'll
give you what you want. You won't need anyone else."

"Only you." The words were a small, sweet cry
from far back in her throat as she clung to him.

He'd wanted to take this slowly, Garth reminded
himself. But he knew now that he wasn't going to be
able to have that luxury, at least not this first time.

"You're so ready for me," he whispered, sucking in
his breath very deeply as he touched the throbbing
core of her desire with trembling fingers. "Do you really want me so much?"

"Please, Garth. I've never wanted anything this
much."

He believed her and the knowledge made his head
spin. Carefully he pushed her legs farther apart, and
she willingly allowed him more intimate access. He
knew that right now she would deny him nothing. The
hunger was a raging fire in him, and Garth could wait

no longer. He slid between her legs, glorying in the feel of her smooth thighs on his own rough-textured skin. The contrast heightened his awareness of her essential femininity to the point that he could barely control himself.

Shannon's arms went around him as she felt him surge against her. She pulled him to her, murmuring her need. His hard body pushed against the damp, dark, velvet of her, making her gasp and then he was inside, burying himself to the hilt in a single, powerful thrust. Her body went suddenly taut, as if reacting to an invasion. The startling change from insistent need to a feeling of fullness and tension took Shannon by surprise.

"Oh, Garth!"

"It's all right, sweetheart. It's all right." He stroked the tangled hair back from her face, his eyes meeting hers. "I'll give you time. You're so small and tight. I didn't realize . . ."

She wanted to laugh but her emotions were too precariously balanced on the knife-edge of passion to allow the humorous release. "It's not me, it's you. You're too big!"

He groaned, covering her mouth with his own. "No. We're both just right," he said against her lips, and then his tongue was sliding between her teeth to establish a rhythm he soon began imitating with his lower body.

Shannon's own body quickly accepted the dominating cadence. She clung to him, her hips rising to meet his, her muscles stretching and contracting deliciously with each thrust. She closed her eyes, giving herself up to the moment and the man. There had never been another night such as this, and she would take all it had to offer.

Time seemed to compress itself, locking out everything except the shimmering passion that gripped Shannon and the man who held her. She felt her senses leaping toward a final precipice of sensation that contained a mystery she'd never fully explored. Eagerly she gave herself to Garth, knowing he could show her the wonders that awaited.

When the sensual ripples of bursting tension finally stormed through her, Shannon cried out and the name that was on her lips as she gasped in astonished release was Garth's.

He heard it, and it was all that was needed to pull him after her into the shuddering finale. His body went rigid, and Shannon heard her own name sounding like torn silk in her ears. Then Garth was collapsing heavily along her body, his weight crushing her into the sheets. A piercingly sweet lethargy enveloped them both.

Several minutes later Shannon became aware of Garth's hand moving idly on the curve of her hip. She opened her eyes and found him looking at her. Tremulously she smiled.

Garth eased himself reluctantly to the side, cradling her in one arm. "You and I," he said very calmly, "have a few things to discuss."

She blinked, mildly confused. "Such as?" He seemed to have returned to full awareness much more quickly than she had.

"Such as making this a habit. I think I'm already an addict."

Shannon relaxed against him. "I'm glad."

Garth yawned. "I've got to go back to San Jose in a couple of days."

Shannon felt herself tensing. "I'd rather not talk about your leaving, Garth. Not tonight."

He smiled lightly, looking both indulgent and amused. "How about discussing the subject of my return?"

Her eyes were alive with happiness. "Is the subject open for discussion?"

"You know I'm going to be back, don't you?"

"When?"

"On the weekend. And the weekend after that and the one after that and the one after that."

"You've rented the cottage for a whole series of weekends?"

"No. I only rented the cottage for a few days. The next time I come over to the coast I'll be staying here with you. Assuming I've got an invitation."

"Oh, Garth, you know you do." She snuggled against him, her happiness threatening to swamp her.

"I didn't expect this, Shannon," he said very thoughtfully.

"Neither did I."

He gave her a small shake. "I'm serious. This changes a lot of things. I'll have to make some plans."

"What sort of plans?"

"Don't worry," he said vaguely. "I'll take care of everything. As long as I know you're waiting here on the weekends, I can handle the details."

The weekends, Shannon thought. She wondered why the phrase bothered her. Of course, for the immediate future the weekends were the only times they would be able to get together. After all, Garth had his company to run in San Jose, and she had her work here on the coast. It was only logical that he should talk in terms of seeing her on the weekends. But something about the way he said it bothered her. She wasn't certain why. It was as if Garth was thinking of her as something separate and distinct from the rest of his life. Someone he saw *only* on the weekends.

Shannon frowned in the darkness and pushed aside the odd, uneasy sensation his words had caused. She was imagining things. Tonight was very special, and she wasn't going to ruin it with feminine paranoia. Deliberately she trailed her fingertips through the curling hair on Garth's chest.

"Hey, that tickles," he complained with a small chuckle.

"What, this?" She traced a circle around one flat, male nipple. "Or this?" She drew her nails lightly down across his stomach. He clamped a hand over her roving hand.

"Didn't your mother ever warn you about what happens when you tease a man?"

"I don't think so. My mother left most of my sex education to the schools. My teachers stuck to little charts and diagrams. I don't recall them discussing teasing."

"Then allow me to complete your education." He rolled over, sprawling on top of her and pinned her wrists above her head. "Women who tease men are liable to find themselves in just this sort of situation." Keeping her hands locked above her head, he began dropping a string of small, nipping kisses across her shoulders and down to the peaks of her breasts.

Shannon shivered. "I can see my mother and the teachers all overlooked something very important."

"It's all right. I don't mind the fact that you've had a limited education. I'm a very patient man, and I'm willing to teach you a few things myself." He used one hand to maintain his hold on her wrists and then began to use his other hand on her body. When he caressed her from her breast to her hip, Shannon gave another small shiver.

"I get the feeling teasing brings its own rewards," she taunted, her hazel eyes full of sensual laughter.

"You think so?" He drew delicate, tantalizing circles on her hip until she moved a little under him. Then he began weaving the same patterns on the inside of her leg. Shannon shifted again, her senses bubbling back into full awareness.

"Garth?"

"Hmm?" He was drawing the patterns higher now, very near the place that sheltered her feminine secrets.

"I think I'm ready for the reward."

"Convince me."

"Let go of my hands and I will," she promised, her voice growing husky with her rising passion. She broke off to gasp as he did something very special and a little mind-shattering with his fingers. "Garth!"

"I'm not convinced."

He continued to hold her wrists gently captive while she began to writhe beneath him. His hand moved more boldly on her until she was begging him to take her again. He listened to her soft pleas, all the while tormenting her so deliciously that Shannon began to think she would go crazy.

"Garth, I . . . Oh, my God, *Garth*!" Her eyes widened in astonishment as he deftly brought her to another nerve-thrilling sense of fulfillment. Only then did he release her wrists, and Shannon instantly wrapped her arms around him, holding him tightly as she trembled beneath him. When a moment had passed, she turned her head and kissed the skin on his shoulder. "Definitely cruel and unusual punishment. I must remember to try teasing you again sometime."

He grinned, his expression relaxed and unabashedly satisfied. "Anytime, honey. I'll look forward to it every weekend."

THE NEXT FEW DAYS passed in a haze of happiness for Shannon. She continued with her work during the hours when Garth disappeared inside his own cottage to pore over his bid proposal papers, but every free moment for both of them was spent together. They took long walks on the beach, walked into town for groceries and Shannon's mail and ate dinner in Shannon's cottage. After dinner Shannon served brandy and turned on the stereo. When Garth reached for her, she went into his arms with the eagerness of a homing pigeon.

When the morning arrived that Garth was due to leave for San Jose, Shannon stood beside the Porsche to say goodbye. Her eyes were suspiciously bright, although she kept her smile very much in place. Garth took her in his arms.

"I'll call you tonight," he said into her hair.

"Good." She sniffed.

"Hey, don't cry," he murmured. "I'm going to be back next weekend, remember?"

"Please don't forget to come back, Garth," she said very seriously.

"I couldn't forget," he replied simply. "I need you too much." He kissed her once more and then he got into the Porsche. "I'll leave work early Friday afternoon."

"It's a long drive," Shannon pointed out, thinking how easy it would be for him to change his mind about making such a long trip after a busy week.

"I don't mind. You'll be waiting at the end of it, won't you?" It wasn't so much a question as a statement of fact.

Shannon nodded. "I'll be waiting."

"That's all I need to know." He glanced across the driveway to where her little red Fiat sat. Garth's brows came together in a thoughtful frown. "I'm not sure I like the idea of you running around in such a small car. You'd be safer in a bigger vehicle."

"Are all Porsche drivers so condescending toward other sports cars?" Shannon teased.

"It's not a question of being condescending," Garth began firmly. "It's just that I think you'd be better protected in a larger car." His expression cleared. "Never mind. We'll talk about it later. Take care, Shannon. I'll be back soon. Be here for me."

Shannon smiled mistily and waved as the Porsche roared out of the driveway. She would be waiting. For a brief, unhappy moment she wondered again about what it was going to be like conducting a weekend affair. She knew she was falling in love with Garth Sheridan.

Shannon had always imagined that love would be a sharing kind of emotion and would of necessity involve a sharing of day-to-day lives as well as the sharing of passion.

She turned back to her cottage, telling herself that it would all work out in the end. Her relationship with Garth was at the very beginning stages. There was plenty of time to hammer out the logistical details. In the meantime she had her work. The buyer from the San Francisco boutique would be arriving the following week and she still had several more sample tote bags to print.

Her heart lightened as she opened the door of her studio and began organizing her printing preparations. She had her work and next weekend she would have her lover. Life was good.

ON FRIDAY MORNING Garth was aware of being nearly consumed by his need to be on the road. Outside his office window, San Jose baked in the smoggy heat of a summer's day. All he had been able to think about since he'd gotten out of bed this morning was driving to the coast. With any luck he'd get out of the Sheri-lectronics office after lunch. God knew he'd spent enough late nights behind his desk this past week to justify an early departure. Shannon was going to wait dinner for him. She had told him so on the phone last night.

Garth closed his eyes and allowed himself the luxury of thinking of Shannon and the coming weekend for a brief moment. The truth was, he always seemed to be thinking about that subject even when his attention was on work. With his customary self-discipline, however, he generally managed to keep the image pushed back to the edge of his awareness where it couldn't get in the way of his getting done what had to be done. Shannon was in a separate compartment from the rest of his life, and he fully intended to keep her there.

Garth had no intention of letting Shannon get mixed up with the side of his life that revolved around work. It suited him perfectly that she lived a safe distance from San Jose and thus a safe distance from the occasionally subtle, often blatant warfare that defined business between Sherilectronics and its competitors in the Silicon jungle. Shannon was too gentle and too unsophisticated to live in his world, Garth decided. Her artistic nature needed protection. He would protect her from his world and in the process he would create a refuge for himself. He might be capable of surviving here, but for the past several months Garth knew he had been questioning the effort it took. A weekend escape to Shannon's softness and warmth sounded more inviting than he could have imagined.

The door opened just as he was sneaking another glance at the clock. His secretary, Bonnie Garnett, smiled her standard professional smile. Bonnie always smiled when she was supposed to smile. Occasionally Garth wondered what she was really thinking behind that cover-girl perfection. She was about the same age as Shannon, but the two women couldn't have been more different. In the five years she had worked for him, Garth had never seen Bonnie when she didn't look as if she could have stepped in front of a fashion photographer's camera. Garth realized how much he liked Shannon's jeans and windblown hair.

"Mr. McIntyre is here to see you, sir. He has the next section of the Carstairs proposal ready for you."

"Fine. Send him in, Bonnie." Reluctantly Garth let the image of the coming weekend slide once again to the back of his mind. "Oh, and Bonnie, I'll be leaving early this afternoon. Was there anything crucial on the agenda?"

"No, sir. I got another call from Mr. Hutchinson's secretary, however, reminding you to keep the twentieth open for the party the Hutchinsons are giving."

Garth impatiently flicked the tip of his pencil on the black glass surface of his desk. He glared at his calendar. "The twentieth is a Saturday."

"That's right. One week from tomorrow."

Garth swore softly. He didn't want to go to the damn party. He rarely attended parties of any kind. But Hutchinson was a longtime business acquaintance, and Garth knew he owed Steve a couple of minor favors. Steve Hutchinson and his wife had both made it clear he could get out of the social debt by attending their one major business party of the year.

The party was going to kick a big hole in a weekend he'd had every intention of sharing with Shannon. Well, he'd cross that bridge when he came to it. Garth tossed the pencil down on the desk. "Send Wes in, Bonnie."

Bonnie's smile didn't waver a fraction in spite of the grim tone in her boss's voice, and Garth knew it was because she was accustomed to the tone. Garth was frequently rather grim. He also paid his secretaries very well. Money, he knew, could buy a great deal of tolerance for grimness.

Wes McIntyre sauntered into the sleekly designed president's office, his own smile casually in place. McIntyre was vice president of corporate strategy, and he'd earned the hard way the position that made him Garth's closest adviser. He was in his early thirties and was the living embodiment of the sun-drenched California look. Blond-haired, blue-eyed and ruggedly handsome, McIntyre was also very sharp when it came to corporate planning. He had a Machiavellian turn of mind that almost matched Garth's. Because he knew how McIntyre's mind worked, Garth trusted his vice president as much as he trusted anyone in the business world. But to be on the safe side, he paid McIntyre very well, too.

"I've finished the scheduling section of the proposal, Garth." Wes took a chrome-and-black-leather chair without being invited. He was sure of his importance in this office. "I don't see any problem telling Carstairs we can have the stuff to them by early spring. It'll mean running some of the assembly lines on an overtime basis, but we can manage."

Garth nodded, satisfied. "Good. Time is as important to Carstairs as price. If we can guarantee delivery by spring, they'll pay for the privilege. Anything else?"

Wes shook his head. "I think that about wraps it up from my end. With the figures you came back with on Monday we should be able to beat any other bid out there. A little fine tuning and the proposal will be ready for Bonnie to type."

"I don't want her doing the job on the word processor. Tell her to use the regular typewriter for the final version of the report, just as she's been doing for the preliminary work. No carbons and no photocopies. And she's to do the whole job herself. No need to drag in any extra clerical help. That's just that many more fingers in the pot."

Wes murmured agreement. "I'll make sure she understands. She's worked here long enough to know that when you slap a Strictly Confidential label on something, you mean business. Hell, the whole company knows it." He grinned. "And if there were a few poor souls who didn't know it, they got the point when you fired George Keller several months ago."

"Keller knew better than to open his mouth about Sherilectronics business at a party. He got what he deserved." Garth closed the folder on his desk. "Okay, that's it, Wes. I'll be gone after lunch. I'll take all the Carstairs bid work papers with me for the weekend, as usual. Everything. I don't want anything left even overnight here in the office."

"Hell, you don't even let those papers lie around the office during lunch hour, let alone overnight or over a weekend! Some folks might call you paranoid." Wes chuckled.

"Some folks might call me careful. I've been burned before. I don't intend to let it happen again. If you need me, you can leave a message with my answering service. I'll get back to you."

"All right." Wes got to his feet and headed for the door. It shut silently behind him.

Garth took one more look at the clock and decided to call it quits. Everything was under control in this world, and all he could think about now was escaping to his other world, the one where the soft, sweet lady in the castle waited for him with open arms.

He stood up and walked to the closet to get his jacket. His bag was already packed and waiting in the Porsche. In a few hours he would be with Shannon. An unaccustomed feeling of elation gripped him.

The pattern of his life had been altered because of what had happened between himself and Shannon last weekend. An endless series of weekend escapes stretched out before him, promising renewal and satisfaction in a world that had nothing to do with the one in which he worked.

Garth promised himself he would do everything in his power to protect his newfound refuge and the woman who maintained it for him. On his way to the door he scooped up the bid package and shoved it into his briefcase.

In his mind he was already nearing Shannon's cottage, anticipating her warm greeting, the good meal she would serve him and the long night ahead in her arms.

It was just barely possible, he thought as he climbed into the Porsche, that with Shannon to go to on the weekends, he might be able to deal with the increasing restlessness he was experiencing these days at work. Knowing that the weekends would bring him the peace and comfort he needed might make it possible for him to work though the strange mood that had been plaguing him for the past few months.

4

GARTH WAS EARLY. She hadn't expected him for another couple of hours. Shannon tossed aside the squeegee as she heard the crunch of tires on gravel accompanied by the well-bred roar of the Porsche engine. Hastily she removed the last greeting card from beneath the silk screen, put it carefully on the drying table and then she raced for the door.

"I didn't expect you until this evening!" she exclaimed, coming quickly down the front steps as Garth climbed out of the Porsche and reached for his leather overnight bag.

"I got away early." He waited for her as she rushed toward him, his eyes warm with a deeply satisfied expression.

Shannon laughed and stopped short just as she was about to throw her arms around him. "I don't dare touch you. I've got paint all over me."

He leaned down and kissed her, something he'd been thinking about doing for the past few hours. A firm, sensually aggressive kiss that contained a wealth of waiting hunger. "Let's go inside. It's been a long trip."

Some of Shannon's pleasure in seeing him faded at the words. "It is a long trip, isn't it? How much time does it take to drive it? Four hours?"

"Almost." He stepped into the cottage and set down the bag. Then he brushed his mouth across hers again, lingeringly this time. "And worth every mile."

"I hope you continue to think so next weekend and the weekend after that." Shannon tried to keep her voice light, but she was afraid some of her uncertainty showed.

"As long as I know you're waiting, I'll be here." Garth hung his jacket up in the hall closet, his actions making him appear very much at home. Then he turned back to her. "Show me what you're doing that's got you covered in red ink."

Shannon's mouth curved again as she led the way to her studio. "I'm screening another order of cards. I was hoping to do some of the totes today, but one of the shops in town called up and said they had to have another order of greeting cards. I was just finishing as you arrived. All I have to do now is clean up." He followed her into the room and stood studying the array of small tools on the worktable, the rack of drying cards that had just received their third and last trip under the silk and the paint-covered squeegee and screen.

"For every color of ink you use in the design on the cards you have to run each one through the process a separate time?" Garth frowned as he examined the screen.

"That's right. I suppose that doesn't seem terribly efficient to someone who runs an electronics firm. I'll bet you crank out fifty billion doohickies an hour on your assembly lines, right?"

"Not quite fifty billion, but I'm sure we get a lot more, er, doohickies out the door than you do cards," he retorted dryly. "Still, I can't market my products as handmade. *Precision* made, yes, but not hand-made."

"What exactly does Sherilectronics make, Garth?" Shannon had been realizing all week how little she still knew of him.

"Circuit boards and other components for companies that manufacture computers," Garth responded absently. He wandered around the room as Shannon began cleaning red ink off the screen. "Nothing that would be of interest to you." He stopped beside a pile of canvas squares. "Are these the designs for the tote bags?"

Shannon glanced over at the pile. "That's right. I wanted to have a variety to show the buyer when she gets here this week."

Garth fingered one of the squares, a brilliantly hued letter *A* decorated with jewel-toned dragons and intricate scrollwork. There was a thoughtful expression on his face. "Will this buyer give you a contract to sign if she decides to buy your totes?"

"Probably," Shannon said carelessly. "I'm sure there will be something in writing about deliveries and prices. Around here I don't worry too much about formal contracts, but I imagine a professional buyer will be used to dealing in a more businesslike manner."

"I'm sure she will. She'll probably also be more accustomed to taking advantage of craftspeople who don't know much about the business world." Garth dropped the canvas he had been holding. "Don't sign anything until I've had a chance to look at it, Shannon."

Shannon looked up in surprise. "But, Garth, that's not necessary. Besides, if she's interested, I'll want to get the deal settled as quickly as possible. This is the first really big buyer I've had. I don't want to do anything to wreck the deal."

"She can wait a few days for the contract. If she were dealing with a large-scale operation, she'd expect to wait awhile. I don't want you signing anything I haven't checked out, honey."

Dismayed, Shannon opened her mouth to argue and then promptly closed it again. Garth was here for such a short time. She didn't want to ruin even a moment of that time by arguing. It occurred to her that this was going to be one of the difficulties with a weekend affair. Problems would be glossed over or ignored because their time together was so limited.

"How was your week?" Shannon asked with what she hoped was a comfortable amount of interest as she finished her cleanup work.

"Long and hectic. I could use a drink. Are you done there?"

She nodded. "I'll change my shirt while you pour us a drink. I've got some wine on the counter."

Garth's mouth crooked as he walked out into the hall and headed for the kitchen. "I brought my own whiskey. Figured you wouldn't have any."

Shannon winced. Next weekend she would be sure to buy some whiskey. She had a lot to learn about Garth, she thought as she went into her bedroom to change into a clean white shirt.

Ice clinked in his whiskey glass as Garth came to stand in her doorway and watch her button her blouse.

Shannon flushed a little under his intent regard. She wasn't accustomed to changing her clothes in front of a man, and the procedure was obviously going to take some getting used to before she could do it nonchalantly. Unobtrusively she turned her back to him and fumbled quickly with the buttons. "How's the bid package going?"

"It'll be ready on time." He sounded totally disinterested in the topic.

Shannon went still as she sensed him moving up behind her. When his hand came down on her shoulder, her fingers came to a halt on one of the buttons. "I see. That...that must be a relief to you. I realize it's very important."

"Is it?" He bent his head and kissed the nape of her neck.

"Well, yes. Garth, I'm interested in your work. I...I really know very little about you. I have a phone number for you in San Jose and that's about it. I don't even know your home address." She shivered slightly as his fingers stroked the curve of her shoulder just inside the blouse.

"I'll make sure you have my address before I leave on Sunday. You can send me one of your handmade cards. Don't worry, Shannon. There's plenty of time to learn all you need to know about me. And as far as my life in San Jose goes, you don't have to worry about learning very much at all. That side of things doesn't have anything to do with us."

It keeps you away from me five days a week, Shannon thought resentfully. But she forced a smile as she turned toward him and wrapped her arms around his waist. "Hungry?"

"Uh-huh. Very." Deliberately he kissed her, parting her lips with his own and amusing himself for a moment by chasing her tongue.

"Then I'd better get dinner in the oven."

"It can wait."

Shannon heard the clink of the glass as he set it down on the dresser and then Garth's fingers were on the buttons she had just fastened. He undid each one and pushed the shirt off her shoulders.

"I like the fact that you don't wear a bra," he said in satisfaction as he cupped her breasts. Then he kissed her slowly again, his thumbs gliding over her nipples. "I've been thinking about you all week, honey. I can't remember a time when a woman filled my thoughts during working hours the way you do. Very distracting."

"I can't imagine anything distracting you."

"Believe me, you've got the power." He pushed her gently toward the bed.

"Garth, what about dinner?"

"What about it? We'll eat it later. Right now I've got another hunger to satisfy. It's been a long week, sweetheart."

She smiled lovingly, framing his face with her hands. "For me, too, Garth."

"I'm glad," he growled as he eased her onto the bed and came down beside her. "I want you as hungry for me as I am for you." His fingers moved over her, seeking the secrets he had uncovered last weekend and glorying in their rediscovery.

Shannon sighed softly, surrendering without further protest to the passion that was already flaring between them. Their time together was so limited, she thought fleetingly. They had to take advantage of every moment. Dinner could wait.

THE WEEKEND SLIPPED PAST all too quickly, just as Shannon had feared. On Sunday morning she stood in the kitchen making coffee while she waited for Garth to get out of the shower and wondered where the time had gone. The week ahead seemed endless. She was going to have to get used to Sundays, she told herself bracingly.

"Smells good," Garth remarked, sauntering into the kitchen and taking a whiff of the coffee. His presence seemed to dominate the cozy room, and Shannon was intensely aware of him. He was still buttoning his shirt, and his hair was damp from the shower. The scene was achingly familiar and yet still strangely alien to her.

"When do you have to leave?" she tried to ask calmly as she poured the coffee. Normally she would have made tea for herself. But Garth preferred coffee.

"I should try to get away around noon. I want to have time this evening to go over some things for my Monday morning meeting with my managers." Garth took a seat at the table and reached for a toast triangle.

"We'll have time for a walk on the beach after breakfast." Determinedly Shannon sought a cheerful comment.

"Sounds good." Garth picked up the coffee mug she set in front of him. "You know, Shannon, I've been thinking about the locks on your doors."

She looked at him in astonishment. "My locks?"

"Yeah. They're lousy. I think I'll get hold of a locksmith in Mendocino or Fort Bragg and have him come out here and secure this place a bit. I worry about you living here by yourself all week long. I'd feel more comfortable if I knew you had some decent locks in the doors and windows."

"Garth, this is a very quiet, very peaceful community. We don't have much crime here. This isn't San Jose."

"I know it isn't San Jose," he said patiently, "but I still don't like the idea of you being here alone."

"I've lived here alone for nearly two years." She was beginning to sound hostile, Shannon realized in horror. She mustn't ruin things. She only had a few more hours with Garth. "I'm sure I'll be fine without new locks."

"I'll phone someone tomorrow. I'll have him contact you and arrange a time to put in the locks."

"Garth, please, I don't need new locks."

He looked at her. "Honey, you're too naive about some of the grim facts of life. But don't worry, I'll take care of everything."

Helplessly Shannon stabbed her fork into a bowl of strawberries. She knew she was feeling resentful, but she didn't dare say anything more. Maybe it would be wise to put in new locks. The ones in place now had been here when she'd leased the cottage. Heaven only knew how long they'd been here before that.

But it wasn't the issue of whether she needed new locks that bothered her; it was the way Garth was assuming responsibility for the decision that was annoying her. He was moving more and more into her life, making decisions and offering advice even when it hadn't been requested. The problem was, Shannon realized, the arrangement was not reciprocal. Garth was involving himself in her world, but she still knew next to nothing about his.

"I'll think about the locks," Shannon offered by way of compromise.

Garth lifted his brows, his expression warmly amused. "No, you won't. I'll think about them. Just leave that sort of thing to me, honey. I'm good at handling details."

Shannon's mouth tightened, but she managed to keep quiet.

It wasn't until they were down on the beach half an hour later that she found out about the party. Shannon got the impression Garth wouldn't have mentioned it at all if she hadn't happened to bring up the subject of another Verna Montana play scheduled for the following weekend.

"She's going to do one she's written herself," Shannon explained with a laugh. "Should be fun. It's a satire on yuppies. She's using various and assorted vegetables as her characters."

"Vegetables."

Shannon grinned. "Verna sees vegetables as having very distinctive personalities."

"I suppose we should be grateful it's not going to be a musical. Singing vegetables might be more than I could handle." Garth suddenly frowned, and his hand tightened abruptly around Shannon's. "Oh, hell, I just remembered. I won't be able to come over to the coast next weekend."

Shannon's heart sank. She turned her attention to the far end of the beach. "Work?" she asked neutrally.

"In a way," Garth groaned. "Actually, it's a damn party."

"A party?"

"A business party. Usually I avoid them like the plague, but this one is being put on by a guy who's done me some favors. He and his wife throw one event a year, and this year it's scheduled for next Saturday. God knows I'd get out of it if I could. Most of my competitors and several clients will be there. I see enough of that crowd at work. I don't like having to socialize with them."

Shannon took a deep breath and said cautiously, "I could drive down to San Jose next weekend. I'm sure I could find a dress somewhere in my closet. I'll go to the party with you."

"No."

She bit her lip, slightly taken aback by the abrupt refusal. She had been expecting some resistance, but this was more like a stone wall. "I don't mind the drive, Garth."

"I don't want you getting mixed up with that side of my life, Shannon." Garth tugged her to a halt and slipped his hands under the curve of her hair. He brushed his mouth across hers and smiled faintly. "Don't look at me like that. It's for your own good, honey. You wouldn't like the kind of people who will be at that party. Believe me. I don't particularly like them myself. It's going to be strictly business."

"And you don't want me mixed up with your business."

"No. Speaking of your driving, though..." he went on thoughtfully.

Shannon stared at him, confused. "What about my driving?"

"I really think you ought to have a bigger car than that little Fiat. You'd be safer in something that puts more steel around you."

"Garth, we were discussing your plans for the weekend, not my car!"

"There's nothing left to discuss concerning the weekend. But I am going to give your Fiat some more thought."

"How can you object to my driving a sports car when you drive one yourself?" she asked, exasperated and hurt. She wanted to argue about the party, and Garth seemed determined to switch the conversation to the subject of her car.

"It's not the same thing, Shannon." Garth resumed walking, Shannon's hand enfolded in his. "The roads around here are narrow and winding. You don't use your car much but when you do I want you to be safe. How would you like a full-size Buick or Ford?"

"Are you kidding? After driving a Fiat? I'd hate it! Garth, listen to me; my car is just fine. I own it free and clear and I love it. I don't want a new car."

"If you want something foreign we can think about getting you a Mercedes. They're good, solid cars with a lot of steel in them."

Shannon wanted to scream in frustration. It took all her willpower to maintain some semblance of civility. She would *not* ruin these last couple of hours with her lover. "I couldn't possibly afford a Mercedes," she pointed out stiffly.

He squeezed her hand. "You don't have to worry about that end of things. I'll take care of it."

"No." It was her turn to sound rigid. "You aren't going to buy a car for me, Garth."

"Why not?"

She finally lost her temper. "Because I say so, that's why! I will not have you spending that kind of money on me, Garth Sheridan. We're not married, we're just weekend lovers. Don't you understand?"

He halted again, his hands going to her shoulders. "You're the one who doesn't understand yet, Shannon. But you will. Soon." He looked as though he wanted to say something else, but he glanced impatiently at his watch instead. "I've got to leave now. It's almost noon. I'll try to get away early on the Friday after next."

"Garth, wait, we need to talk...."

"I'll call you this evening." He turned and led her back down the beach, and Shannon could see he was already starting to plan ahead again. "Don't forget what I said about any contracts that buyer asks you to sign. Hold on to them until I've had a chance to go over them."

"Garth, I really think I can deal with the matter. I've been supporting myself with my silk-screen products for two years." Frantically Shannon tried to make herself sound reasonable and prudent, but she was aware of an abnormal edge in her voice.

"Just don't sign anything. Oh, and I'll let you know about the locksmith sometime this week."

Shannon gave up for the moment. There was no sense arguing now. Time had run out and the weekend was over. A few minutes later she stood in the driveway watching the Porsche leave once more for San Jose. She felt as if Garth were leaving for another world, not just another town. The gulf between herself and her weekend lover suddenly seemed very wide.

Frustrated and uncertain, Shannon went back inside the cottage. It was difficult to remember that she was the one who had first approached Garth. She was no longer certain of what she had started by her impulsiveness that day on the beach when she had followed him into the fog and invited him to dinner. The busy, settled routine of her life had been turned upside down, and she wasn't at all sure how to right it.

The dark, brooding quality that had compelled her to push until she learned more about him was still a part of Garth. She still didn't know what secrets it shrouded, although she was beginning to get an intuitive feel for some of them. She could hazard a guess, for instance, that once he had decided to plunge into an affair, Garth's first instincts were to keep his private life and his business life carefully separated. She wondered where he'd learned to be so wary of mixing the two.

His tendency to start making some of the major decisions in her life seemed to stem from a sense of over-protectiveness. It might just as easily be a function of his normal take-charge attitude, however. Shannon thought about that as she wandered back into her studio. The man was accustomed to running his own company. Taking charge came naturally to him. But it was more than that. The things he was concerning himself with in her life were directly related to what he saw as being important to her safety and welfare. He wanted better locks on her cottage, a safer car for her to drive and he was convinced she couldn't handle the business side of her own life.

Shannon sat down at the worktable and examined the sketches she had been making for a stencil pattern for Annie O'Connor's baby crib. She had promised Annie she'd have some of the alphabet stencils cut by Monday. She had better get busy. Shannon picked up her sketching pen and went to work. She tried not to think about the future. She would take the weekends one at a time. There wasn't much else she could do, because she knew for certain she was in love with her weekend lover.

THE BUYER from Lost and Found arrived as promised on Wednesday morning. Shannon nervously watched her get out of the car. The woman looked very San Francisco. Short, stylish hair, narrow skirt, padded-shouldered silk blouse and high heels. Very trendy and very sophisticated. All of a sudden Shannon wondered what this stylish creature saw in a bunch of handcrafted tote bags. It was very daunting. But her fears vanished almost at once as the woman exclaimed over the designs.

"They're absolutely marvelous! Wonderful! I haven't seen anything like them anywhere and, of course, that's the whole point, isn't it? Lost and Found customers will love them. How many can you give me a month?"

Shannon tried not to exhibit her excitement and tension. "Would twenty a month sound reasonable?"

"I could use fifty."

"Do you really think so?"

The buyer nodded with absolute certainty. "At least. More if you can get them done. What's your production schedule?"

Belatedly Shannon remembered Garth's advice to sound positive and businesslike about production schedules. "It can be adjusted to suit demand. I have someone who will work part-time as needed to finish the bags. I'll handle the actual silk-screening process myself, of course. I think we could manage fifty." Mentally she crossed her fingers behind her back.

"Excellent. I've brought a contract with me. Just a formality, you understand. Keeps everything neat and legal. We'll go over it during lunch, and I'll explain the highlights. I can take you to lunch, can't I? You'll have to suggest someplace in the area. I haven't been over to the coast in ages."

"Sure." Shannon sucked in her breath at the rapidity with which everything was moving. Maybe there was a little too much speed involved here. The mention of the contract had been very fleeting. What was it Garth had said about big-city buyers taking advantage of naive craftspeople? "I'll, uh, want some time to look over the contract, if you don't mind."

"Oh, it's a very simple one. Nothing to it."

"All the same, it will take me a little time to study it." Before the buyer could argue the matter, Shannon waved a hand around the studio. "Would you like me to explain what goes on here?"

"Oh, definitely. What are those?"

"Greeting cards. I sell them locally."

The buyer frowned over a stack of boxed cards. "I like the bird design and the flowers, but I love the illuminated letters. They're absolutely exquisite. I wonder if I shouldn't place an order for a few boxes and see how they do in the store."

Shannon began to feel overwhelmed. "I didn't know you sold cards in the Lost and Found."

"Normally we don't, but these are very special and they might do very well next to the totes." The buyer smiled brilliantly. "Let me have that guided tour."

It was nearly seven o'clock that night when Shannon finally sank into a chair with a glass of wine and dialed Garth's home number. She couldn't wait to tell him the news. On the table beside her sat the unsigned contract. Shannon had convinced the buyer to leave it with her for a while, promising to mail it as soon as possible. The woman hadn't been pleased, but she was a businesswoman and quickly accepted the inevitable. She wanted the totes.

The phone rang six times in Garth's home before Shannon admitted to herself he wasn't there. Her fingers drummed restlessly on the arm of the chair as she considered where he might be. Realistically speaking he could be anywhere, including out with another woman.

Shannon thought about that as she closed her eyes and leaned her head back against the chair. She knew so little about Garth. It was entirely possible he kept a wife and ten kids in San Jose. She smiled to herself at the thought. No, whatever Garth might be doing at this hour of the night, he wasn't two-timing her. At least not with another woman. She trusted him.

But she wasn't at all sure she trusted the business side of his life. On a hunch, Shannon picked up the receiver again and dialed the number for Sherilectronics. She wasn't really surprised when the phone was answered promptly by a professional-sounding female voice.

"Sherilectronics, can I help you?"

At seven o'clock at night, no less. Shannon marveled at the late hours. She wondered what Garth had to pay in overtime to get a secretary who sounded this professional at this hour. She tried to conjure up an image of the woman and failed. It made her realize again how many gaps there were in her knowledge of Garth.

"I was calling to speak to Mr. Sheridan. Is he there?"

"He's here, but he's in a meeting. If you'll leave your name and number, I'll have him return your call."

Thoroughly intimidated by the notion of pulling Garth out of a late meeting, Shannon hastily apologized. "That's all right. Just tell him Shannon Raine called. It's nothing crucial. I'll contact him later."

"Hold on a moment, Miss Raine. I have instructions to put through any call from you."

"No, wait, that's all right—" Shannon said quickly, but it was too late. There was an abrupt silence and then a man's voice, sounding harried and impatient came on the line. "Sheridan's office. What's up?"

"I'm sorry," Shannon said, annoyed with herself for apologizing yet again. "This is Shannon Raine. I was calling for Garth, but I understand he's busy and I don't want to interrupt."

A hand was clamped over the mouthpiece on the other end of the line, and Shannon heard the man's muffled voice speaking to someone else. "It's somebody called Shannon Raine. Want me to get rid of her, Garth?"

Garth's voice sounded in the distance. "Hell, no, let me have that, Wes." A second later, he was on the line. "Shannon? What's wrong?"

"Nothing's wrong. I'm sorry I bothered you, Garth." Shannon felt distinctly like an intruder who had blundered into Garth's other world without invitation. "I tried to tell everyone I'd get hold of you later, but they put me through and I—"

He cut through the flow of apologetic words. "It's all right, honey. I've told my secretary to put through your calls. What did you want?"

Her news seemed very trivial now. "I just wanted to tell you about the buyer's visit today. But it can wait."

"How did it go?"

Shannon relaxed a little at the genuine interest in his voice. "Really well, Garth. She loved the totes, and she even wants some of the cards."

"That's wonderful. Did she leave a contract?"

"It's right here in front of me." Shannon glanced uneasily at the three-part document lying on the table.

"Fine. Don't sign anything until I get over there."

Shannon sighed, too elated by the buyer's visit to argue. "All right, Garth." She paused. "Are you going to be working much later tonight?"

"We're getting some last-minute sections of a proposal ready. I'll probably be here until nine or ten."

"Oh." She was shocked but tried not to show it. "Well, I'm sorry to have bothered you," she heard herself say.

"It's all right, honey." But she could hear the impatience in his voice. He had a lot of work ahead of him tonight, and he wanted to get back to it. "Congratulations on your big sale. I'll call you tomorrow, and we'll discuss it further."

"Fine. Good night, Garth." Shannon hung up the phone wishing she'd never had the urge to call his office.

She was an intruder there. There was no doubt about it, regardless of how polite people were when she called. She didn't even know the name of Garth's secretary or how close the man called Wes was to him. She knew so damn little about Garth Sheridan's other life, and he seemed very unwilling to share it with her.

Next weekend the business side of his life would steal even the short time she might normally have had with Garth. Shannon was filled with both curiosity and resentment. Underneath both of those emotions was a vague fear she didn't want to put into words. Shannon sat thinking about her options for a long time before she began to gather her courage and make her plans.

She knew intuitively that if her relationship with Garth was ever to get beyond the weekend-affair stage, she was going to have to see and understand the business side of his life. He had to be convinced to share it with her. She could not let him isolate her from it forever.

Somehow she had to gently force him to share his world with her. Shannon made her decision. She would find a way to attend that party in San Jose with Garth, even if it meant taking him by surprise.

5

THE PARKING LOT of the Sherilectronics building was absorbing the summer heat and sending it back into the atmosphere in muggy waves. Shannon had spent the last hundred miles of the drive from the Mendocino coast wishing she'd had air-conditioning in the Fiat. She was nervous enough about the coming confrontation; she hadn't needed the added perspiration problems caused by the heat.

The lot was nearly empty, but in addition to Garth's Porsche parked near the main entrance, there was a handful of other cars. Shannon grabbed her tote bag and climbed out of the Fiat feeling damp and rumpled. The long, peach-colored cotton skirt and matching loose-fitting blouse were both badly wrinkled. When she had pulled them out of the back of her closet this morning, she had thought they looked just right for a warm summer's day, very breezy and carefree. Disgustedly she paused to try smoothing the fabric a bit before heading toward the glass wall of doors. Then she bent to check her hair in the side mirror. At least it didn't look as if it had just come out of a steam room.

Straightening, Shannon examined the angled-glass-and-steel structure in front of her. The name Sherilectronics on the front was done in a hard-edged script that was reminiscent of a computer printout. The building was three stories high and seemed to be entirely occupied by Garth's company. There were other structures nearby, done in the same cold, modern industrial style and they all had signs declaring that they, too, were part of the computer revolution. Together they formed what was called an industrial park. Shannon couldn't see anything parklike about the acres of high-tech industry that surrounded her, unless she counted the few trees planted along the sidewalks.

Her first impression of Garth's world confirmed her worst fears. It looked very alien.

When she discovered a uniformed guard at the entrance of Sherilectronics, Shannon knew she was definitely in another world. He was very polite but very firm. The name Balley Security Services was embroidered over his left pocket.

"Can I help you, ma'am?"

"I'm here to see Mr. Sheridan," Shannon admitted self-consciously.

"Is he expecting you?"

"Well, no, but I don't think he'll mind." *Much.*

"I'll call up to the office for you," the guard said pleasantly. "This is Saturday, so the receptionist isn't on duty. Have a seat." He gestured toward a lobby chair.

This wasn't quite the way Shannon had planned it. "Couldn't I just go on up and surprise him?"

The guard looked at her with a wry expression and shook his head. "Afraid not. Mr. Sheridan doesn't like surprises. That's why he hires people from my firm to stand here at the front door. May I have your name?"

"Shannon Raine." She hitched her tote bag onto her shoulder and decided to wait standing up. Sitting down would just add a few more wrinkles to the cotton skirt. Tensely she listened while the guard contacted Garth's office.

"Bonnie, there's a Miss Raine here to see Mr. Sheridan. Shall I send her up?" There was a pause while the guard politely scrutinized his guest. "Okay, fine." He hung up the phone. "Third elevator, top floor. Sheridan's secretary said you're to go straight up."

Shannon nodded and started for the elevator. Even now the mysterious Bonnie would be telling Garth he was about to receive a visitor. Shannon's palms went damp as she rode the elevator alone to the third floor.

When the doors hissed open she found herself in another spacious lobby. In the center of it sat a striking woman who could have just stepped out of *Vogue* magazine. The smile she gave Shannon was as perfect as the rest of her. She probably typed a thousand words a minute, too, Shannon thought with a sigh. The woman looked competent as well as beautiful. The name on the discreet plate in front of her was Bonnie Garnett.

"Miss Raine? I'll tell Mr. Sheridan you're here."

Shannon clutched her tote. "He doesn't know yet?" For some reason she felt as if she'd received a small reprieve.

Bonnie shook her head. "He's in a meeting with Mr. McIntyre. They've been at it since seven o'clock this morning." She leaned forward and touched a small button on the intercom. "Mr. Sheridan, you have a visitor. A Miss Raine."

Shannon realized she was holding her breath waiting for the response. The pause before Garth answered seemed to last a hundred years. When it came his voice sounded so cold and devoid of emotion that Shannon nearly lost her nerve entirely.

"I'll be right out, Bonnie."

Bonnie released the intercom button and gave Shannon another of her perfect smiles. Her eyes slipped to the tote and suddenly there was more than professional interest in her gaze. "What a lovely bag. Where did you get it?"

"I, uh, made it." Shannon smiled weakly. The door to the inner office remained ominously closed.

Bonnie got up from behind her desk and came around the corner. "May I see it? I've never seen anything quite like it."

Obediently Shannon extended the large tote. Bonnie's interest took Shannon's mind off the door to the inner office. "It's a silk-screen process. I brought a few of my totes along with me on this trip just in case I decide to stay through Monday or Tuesday. I thought I might be able to pay some calls on some potential buyers here in San Jose." It had seemed a reasonable idea at the time. Now Shannon wasn't so certain.

"You designed this?" Bonnie touched the brilliantly hued decorated letter *R* on the side of the canvas tote. "It looks like something out of a medieval manuscript. One of those old, illuminated pages. It's fantastic. I'd give my word processor to have one."

Some of Shannon's self-assurance returned as she saw the genuine appreciation on Bonnie's face. "Well, as it happens, I've got one with a *B* on it downstairs in the car. Would you like to see it?"

"I'd love to see it. But I suppose they're awfully expensive," Bonnie added regretfully.

"Oh, I wouldn't sell it to you. It would be a gift. I mean, you're Garth's secretary and . . . and I'm sure you're a friend of his, too, and I wouldn't dream of selling anything to a friend. I'll just run down to the car and—" Shannon broke off abruptly as the door across the room opened silently, framing Garth. She had never been more aware of the chilly color of his gray eyes. They were pools of ice today. Her fingers tightened around the strap of the tote bag.

"Hello, Shannon. I wasn't expecting you."

She sucked in her breath, realizing that in the back of her mind she'd been hoping that he'd at least greet her with a kiss. Managing a small, uncertain smile, she faced him. "I decided to surprise you and drive down for the party tonight." Summoning up all her courage, she walked across the room and lifted her face for his kiss. She waited with a pounding heart to see if he would embarrass her in front of Bonnie and the man behind him in the office.

There was a tense moment while Garth simply looked down at her. She couldn't begin to guess what he was thinking, but Shannon knew he wasn't pleased. Then, to her intense relief, he lowered his head and kissed her briefly. It wasn't exactly a lover's greeting, she decided bleakly, but at least he hadn't sent her packing on the spot.

"A surprise, hmm?" He shook his head once. "I should have guessed you'd pull something like this. Wes, this is Shannon Raine." Garth made the introduction without taking his eyes off Shannon.

Wes McIntyre came forward, extending his hand and a warm, friendly smile. "I'm pleased to meet you, Shannon. Have a long drive?"

Grateful for the easy, cheerful greeting, Shannon grinned ruefully. "No air-conditioning in my car. It shows. I'd forgotten how warm it can get over here."

"Where are you from?"

"The coast. Near Mendocino."

"Great country," Wes said, looking wistful. "Sounds especially good on a day like this."

Bonnie stepped forward and began chatting in a bright, friendly manner. It occurred to Shannon that the secretary and Wes were both doing their best to cover up Garth's cool, remote manner. She was increasingly grateful to both of them.

"Shannon made that tote bag, Wes. Isn't it fantastic? Most unusual accessory I've seen in a long time.

She says she has one down in the car that has a *B* on it. I was just about to beg for it when you and Mr. Sheridan opened the door."

"Very interesting," Wes said, admiring the bag. "It's different. What's the process?"

"Silk-screening," Shannon told him and plunged into a detailed discussion of how she created the designs. Anything was better than having Garth stand there looking at her as if he didn't know what to do with her. But even as she began a description of the design process, Garth apparently came to a decision about what to do next.

"It's almost lunchtime," he announced, glancing at the stainless-steel watch on his wrist. He began rolling down the sleeves of his shirt and fastening the cuffs. "Bonnie, you and Wes grab a bite to eat. I'll take Shannon out for a meal and meet both of you back here in an hour."

"Sure," Wes said, just as if the words hadn't constituted an order. "Come on, Bonnie, I'll treat you to a Monster Burger."

Bonnie laughed, her beautiful eyes lighting with real pleasure. "The last of the big spenders."

"Hey, I work for Garth Sheridan. That's big-time, baby. Only the best for you."

Wes took Bonnie's arm in a familiar fashion and led her toward the elevator. When it closed behind them, Shannon risked an amused glance in Garth's direction. "I sense an office romance in bloom."

Garth shrugged. "As long as they keep it out of the office, I don't give a damn. Let's go." Shannon got a glimpse of papers scattered across a glass-topped desk before Garth closed the door to his inner office, locked it and then took Shannon's arm.

The ride down in the elevator was completed in silence. Garth didn't say anything at all until he caught sight of the little red Fiat sitting near his Porsche. "You really like to live dangerously, don't you? Two hundred miles in that thing?"

Shannon didn't respond as she allowed herself to be seated in the Porsche. She stared gloomily at the telephone installed on the driver's side. Garth had said he didn't consider his car a luxury. Maybe having a phone in it made it a business expense as far as he was concerned. A moment later Garth slid in beside her, filling the car with his dominating presence. She still wasn't sure of his mood.

"I had to come, Garth."

He backed the Porsche out of its slot. "Why?"

"Because it was beginning to look as if you would never invite me, and I wasn't content to know only the side of you that you planned to let me see on the weekends." She turned in the seat, her fingers digging into the fabric of the tote bag on her lap. "Admit it, you probably never would have invited me to San Jose, would you?"

"Probably not. There's no need. You don't belong here."

"Why not?"

"Hell, it's hard to explain. Let's just say I don't want you mixed up with the kind of people who will be at the party tonight. It's not going to be your kind of crowd, Shannon. My working world isn't a very nice one, and I didn't want you getting involved with it."

"Garth, I'm not completely naive. I'm also not a silly, empty-headed female or an artist who's incapable of dealing with the real world. You don't have to protect me. Ever since we started this relationship you've been laying down rules and marking off boundaries that I'm not to cross. You were making it very clear that I'm to stay confined to my cottage on the coast and wait dutifully for you to arrive on the weekends. Then I find out I'm not even going to get every weekend with you. Your social life here in San Jose takes precedence. Did you really expect me to get involved in a serious relationship that operates on that kind of basis? I tried to adjust for a while, Garth, but I've decided it's not going to work. If that's what you want, you're going to have to find another woman."

Garth shifted gears with a smooth, savage movement. "So you decided to drive over to San Jose this weekend and throw down the gauntlet, is that it?"

Shannon sighed, collapsing back against the seat. "I was hoping you'd realize how ridiculous it is to try to keep me confined to just a tiny corner of your life."

There was a taut silence, and then Garth said quietly, "I don't know why I keep forgetting how persistent you can be when you make up your mind. All right, Shannon. You're here. There's not much I can do about it now. We'll go to the party tonight, and tomorrow we'll talk about how this relationship is going to operate in the future."

Shannon studied his profile, unable to determine whether she had won or lost the battle. One step at a time, she told herself bracingly. Risking a small smile, she tried to put the conversation onto a more neutral subject.

"Are you and Wes McIntyre still working on that bid proposal for Carstairs?"

"That's right. Bonnie's typing the final version today. It goes to Carstairs in another week or so. We're finishing it in plenty of time." Garth kept his answers clipped as he nosed the Porsche into the parking lot of a small restaurant.

"I like Bonnie," Shannon ventured.

"She's a first-class secretary." Garth seemed to think that said it all. He led the way toward the restaurant.

"If she's the one typing your precious bid proposal, you must trust her as much as you trust McIntyre."

"I suppose so," Garth said offhandedly as he and Shannon stepped inside the air-conditioned restaurant. "Unfortunately, you can't do business efficiently unless you let a few key people in on all the facts. But I take as many precautions as possible. That bid package doesn't leave my office except in my briefcase. There are no copies."

Shannon shot him a curious glance. "If you had your choice, you'd keep everything to yourself and not trust anyone, right?"

"Life works better that way."

"Where did you learn to be so paranoid, Garth?"

"I'm not paranoid, I'm realistic. After you've met a few of my social acquaintances tonight, maybe you'll see why."

IT WASN'T HARD to spot the Hutchinsons' home. The Ferraris and Porsches were parked in two gleaming rows along the curbs for over a block. Shannon looked at them in amused awe as Garth slid his car into a spot at the end of one line.

"Does everyone in Silicon Valley drive a Ferrari or a Porsche?"

"The Ferrari is actually the preferred car," Garth told her dryly. "Driving one implies the owner has just gone public with the stock in his firm and is now a very important computer wizard. Porsches are for us more staid types." He opened the door on her side and helped her out. "All right, let's get this over with."

"We're supposed to be going to a party, Garth, not our doom."

"Planning to enjoy yourself?" His gaze moved over her slim dress of yellow silk. It had a scooped neck, puffed sleeves and it was patterned with colorful flowers around the hem. Shannon had paired it with yellow high-heeled sandals and a simple gold necklace. She carried one of her exquisite tote bags, which somehow went as beautifully with the silk dress as it did with jeans. Garth had never seen Shannon dressed like this. He had been eyeing her covertly ever since she had emerged from the bedroom of the house. He was aware of the fact that even though he was apprehensive about the evening ahead, he was, nevertheless, almost fiercely proud of her. She was so gloriously different from the vast majority of women he knew.

The sophistication of the dress was a piquant contrast to the honesty of her smile and the genuine friendliness in her eyes. The combination was inherently dangerous, he realized. There were going to be men here tonight who would find Shannon an amusing challenge. His fingers closed tightly on her elbow as he guided her toward the Hutchinsons' Chinese-red doors, and he wished he and Shannon were back at the coast so that he could indulge her sweet recklessness without fear of the results.

"Of course I'm planning to enjoy myself," she announced breezily as they walked up the tiled steps. "I haven't been to a real party in a long time."

Garth smiled reluctantly, unable to completely resist the cheerful enthusiasm in her. "Stay close to me. I don't want you wandering off by yourself tonight, understand?"

"This isn't a jungle, Garth."

"That's a matter of opinion." He raised his hand to punch the doorbell.

The door was opened a few minutes later by an attractive woman in her late fifties. Her silver hair was cut in the latest style, and her figure in the expensive

red jersey dress could have been that of a much
younger woman. She greeted Garth with delight.

"You made it. Steve and I always wonder when we
issue you an invitation. It's good to see you again,
Garth. And who is this?" She turned brightly to greet
Shannon.

"Shannon Raine. Shannon, this is Ellen Hutchinson. She and her husband, Steve, are our hosts this
evening." Garth didn't release Shannon's arm as he
made the introductions.

"How nice to meet you, my dear. Come on inside.
I'll show you where you can leave your bag, if you like.
It certainly is unusual. Very attractive. We'll just be a
minute, Garth. Steve and the others are out on the
back terrace."

Garth nodded reluctantly as Shannon was swept
down a hall to a bedroom that was obviously serving
as a temporary cloakroom. There were several other
purses on the bed and a few shawls tossed across one
brocade chair.

"I know Garth didn't have a chance to tell you I'd
be coming with him this evening, Mrs. Hutchinson. I
hope I haven't inconvenienced you." Shannon put her
tote down on the bed and turned to her hostess with
a smile.

"I can't tell you how happy we are to have you here
tonight," Ellen Hutchinson declared firmly. "It's good
to see Garth with a nice young woman again. It's like
pulling teeth getting him to mix socially, you know.
Steve and I were fully prepared for him to simply not

show up at all this evening. Garth hates social functions that are in any way related to business. Actually, I'm not sure he really enjoys any kind of social function."

"So I gather."

"It probably has something to do with Christine, of course. Once burned, twice shy and all that." Ellen started toward the door.

"Christine?" Shannon tried to sound casual, as if she couldn't quite place the name.

"His ex-wife. Perhaps he hasn't mentioned her to you?"

"We don't discuss her."

"Not surprising, under the circumstances." Ellen chuckled conspiratorially. "Just between the two of us, you're not at all like her. I never could warm to Christine. Then, when she ran off with James . . ."

This was going too quickly. Shannon coughed a little and cleared her throat. "Garth hasn't told me the story," she said diffidently, feeling she ought to cut off the flow of information.

"Not many men want to explain to a new love that their ex-wife ran off with their best friend. James was not only Garth's friend, they were partners. I really am chatting too much, aren't I? Steve tells me I tend to talk too much, and I'm afraid he's right. It's just that I was really so pleased to see you and Garth here tonight. Come along, Shannon. I want to introduce you to everyone."

The doorbell chimed just as Ellen Hutchinson was guiding Shannon toward the terrace. Ellen paused to open it, took one look at Wes McIntyre accompanied by Bonnie Garnett and laughed. "I think I'm getting behind on the latest style," she announced. "Where is everyone getting those wonderful tote bags?"

Bonnie smiled, glancing down at the tote Shannon had given her after lunch that afternoon. "As far as I know, there's only one other running around San Jose. Hi, Shannon."

"Hello, Bonnie. I'm glad you like the bag."

"I couldn't resist bringing it tonight. It does wonders for this dress."

Shannon was about to reply when Garth's voice sounded from directly behind her. "Here's your drink, Shannon."

She spun around, realizing she hadn't heard his approach. "Thank you, Garth." Demurely she accepted the glass of white wine.

"Come on out on the terrace. You might as well meet a few of these people."

Shannon nodded, ignoring the cool tone of his voice. She sensed the silent tension in him as he casually made introductions to a bewildering variety of people. His possessiveness must have been obvious to the others, she decided. Garth rarely left her side as the party wore on. He hovered over her like a protective hawk, his expression watchful.

On at least three occasions his attitude was even more austere than normal when he made introductions. The first time she noticed it, Shannon turned to look up at Garth as the man she had just met moved off into the crowd.

"What's wrong, Garth?"

"Kenyon's firm is also bidding on the Carstairs contract," he explained grudgingly.

"Oh. He seemed nice enough."

"He'd cut my throat in a dark alley for that contract."

Shannon grinned. "Then you'd better stay out of dark alleys until the bidding is settled."

It was Wes McIntyre who responded to her comment as he wandered over to stand beside Shannon. He cast a half-humorous, half-knowing look at his boss. "If Kenyon has any sense, he'll be the one keeping clear of dark alleys. He's competed against Sherilectronics before. He knows Garth doesn't play games."

"What a cheerful thought." Shannon didn't look at Garth.

A few minutes later she experienced the second overly polite introduction, this time to a pleasant young man who clearly belonged to one of the Ferraris parked outside. When he'd departed in search of another drink, Shannon cocked an eyebrow at Garth.

"Well?" she demanded. "Why the cold shoulder there?"

"Tyler used to work for me. When he got lured away by HiCal, he tried to take several new component designs with him."

Shannon swallowed. "I see."

"He didn't get out the door with them. But just to teach HiCal a lesson, I stole one of their best design engineers."

"A fun business."

On the third occasion she sensed an added coldness in the introductions, Shannon was almost afraid to inquire into the matter. But curiosity overcame good sense.

"Okay," she challenged, "what awful crime did that nice Mr. Eaker commit against Sherilectronics?"

"None."

"Then why all the disdain and disgust?"

"Eaker is presently under investigation by the FBI for his role in a recent sale of restricted electronic parts to a foreign power."

Shannon nearly choked on her wine. "Good lord. A spy? An honest-to-goodness spy?"

"Nothing's been proven yet."

"But you're sure Eaker is involved?"

"It's a good bet. It's also a good bet the FBI won't be able to nail him. He's smart."

"What's he doing at a nice party like this?" Shannon asked, bewildered.

Garth's mouth curved. "As I said, nothing's been proven."

Shannon tried to enjoy herself for the remainder of the evening, but it was difficult. If she smiled too brilliantly at a man, Garth moved in, cutting off whatever conversation had been going on at the time.

When she tried to slip away to pay a visit to the buffet table, Garth followed, handing her a plate to fill for him, too. And on the occasions when the words "Carstairs contract" came up in a discussion, Shannon found herself being led off to join another group.

Her first moment of freedom came when she excused herself to use the powder room. Some places were still sacrosanct, she reflected a few minutes later as she emerged back into the hall. She passed the room that was being used to store purses and shawls and noticed both her own tote and Bonnie's lying on the bed. Amid the clutter of more ordinary leather and fabric bags, the vividly hued designs on the totes were readily visible. Shannon was pleased that Bonnie had liked hers enough to bring it tonight.

As she came around the hall into the white-on-white living room, Shannon was startled to be greeted by a masculine voice.

"Garth finally let you escape, I see." Ed Kenyon was standing beside a huge potted palm, sipping a martini.

Kenyon. The man whose firm was bidding against Garth's for the Carstairs contract. Shannon smiled politely. "He's afraid I'll feel lost among all these strangers."

Kenyon chuckled. He was a good-looking man in his early forties, brown-haired and blue-eyed. He was dressed in an expensive Italian-made summer suit, and Shannon was fairly certain he, too, owned one of the Ferraris out front. "Garth never does anything out of sheer good manners. He's keeping tabs on you because he wants to make it clear you're not available. Can't blame the guy, I guess. Not after the way his first wife skipped with his partner."

Everyone seemed to know about the mysterious Christine and her affair with Garth's friend James. With that kind of scandal hanging around in the background, she could understand why Garth wasn't anxious to introduce another woman to his business acquaintances.

"I'm afraid I'm new in Garth's life. I don't know much about his past. Maybe it's better if I hear the details from him." She nodded serenely and started to step past Ed Kenyon.

He put the hand that wasn't holding the martini glass on the wall beside her shoulder, halting her. "Hey, I'm sorry. Didn't mean to step on any toes. You've got a lot of class, you know that? Garth may have gotten lucky this time around. Look, let's start over. Any friend of Garth's is a friend of mine."

"I understood the two of you were rivals."

Kenyon grinned. "That doesn't mean much. Around here everyone involved in the computer business is a potential rival. I take it you're not from San Jose?"

"No, I'm just visiting from the coast."

"Ah, that explains it." Kenyon nodded wisely, his hand still on the wall next to Shannon.

"Explains what?"

"Why you're under the impression Garth and I are rivals. I suppose he's told you his firm is going to be the one to walk off with that Carstairs contract?"

Shannon moved uneasily, turning slightly to slip away from the restraining hand. "I don't know anything about Garth's business."

"Then you'd better learn, honey. A smart, pretty lady like you needs to know which way to jump when things move. And things do move fast here in the valley. You wouldn't want to be left hanging on to a loser instead of a winner, would you?" Kenyon set down his martini glass and flattened his other palm on the wall beside Shannon's head, blocking the escape route she had been about to take. He leaned close. "Between you and me, Shannon, I'm a winner."

Outrage mingled with disgust in Shannon's mind. She reminded herself that she was a guest at a party and the last thing she wanted to do was create a scene. But this had gone far enough. She lifted her chin and stepped away from the wall, trying to force him to back away from her.

"Excuse me, Mr. Kenyon, Garth's waiting for me."

"Let him wait." His arm still blocked her path, and his blue eyes were taunting.

Shannon took a deep breath and ducked under one restraining arm. She had just slipped out from captivity when she glanced across the room and saw Garth.

"Garth!" She hurried toward him. "I was just coming to look for you."

"Get your bag, Shannon," he ordered, his voice too lethally soft. His eyes were on Kenyon. "We're leaving."

"But, Garth . . ." Helplessly she let her protest run into the ground. She didn't need any extra degree of feminine intuition to tell her this was not a time to try setting the record straight. Garth was furious. The knowledge subdued her. She'd never seen him in this mood and it alarmed her. For a moment she had a mental picture of Kenyon and Garth in a dark alley with knives. It wasn't a pleasant image. She knew the blood on the ground would be Kenyon's.

Choosing discretion as the better part of valor for the moment, Shannon went back down the hall to the bedroom to fetch her tote bag. Sadly she told herself that it was only to be expected that her first major social event shared with Garth turned out to be a disaster. Parties and Garth didn't seem to mix.

6

WHEN SHANNON COULD STAND the awful silence in the Porsche no longer, she set her teeth and muttered, "Just say it and get it over."

"We'll talk when we get home. Right now I've got my hands full with this traffic." Garth downshifted for a light that went green just as he coasted to the white line. With ruthless skill he brought the Porsche back up to speed.

There was a cold, tight energy in his movements that told Shannon all she wanted to know about his mood. Watching him out of the corner of her eye, she kept silent until he had parked the car in the garage of his expensive condominium. When she had first seen his home earlier, Shannon had looked around eagerly, seeking the subtle clues that would tell her more about the man she loved. The condominium complex was starkly modern in design, all angled white walls and endless windows. It was surrounded by a great deal of perfect green lawn and several rows of exotic shrubs. There were the usual California-style pool and athletic facilities in the center of the grounds.

The inside of Garth's home was as cool and uncluttered looking as the outside. It was a little too uncluttered for Shannon's taste. The place reminded her of his office. The furnishings were composed of sleek leather-and-steel pieces with accents of black glass. The windows in the living room and bedroom opened onto Japanese-style gardens that were maintained by professional gardeners and looked it. Shannon couldn't imagine having a comfortable picnic in such a perfect garden.

Tonight as she walked into the condo, Shannon was suddenly aware of the fact that she felt like an errant wife. It was a ridiculous feeling, under the circumstances, and she resented it. Lifting her chin, she tossed the tote bag onto the gray carpet beside the nearest chair and turned to face Garth.

He ignored her, pacing across the room to the liquor cabinet. Without a word he poured himself a shot of whiskey.

"All right, Garth. Let's get this out in the open," Shannon said, all her tension and uncertainty making her sound quite aggressive. "I don't particularly appreciate being made to feel like a stupid little fool who can't handle herself in a difficult social situation."

Garth leaned back against the black steel cabinet and glanced down at the whiskey in his glass. When he looked up, his eyes were the color of ice. "'A difficult social situation,'" he repeated slowly. "Is that what you call getting yourself cornered by my chief rival?"

"This may come as a shock, Garth, but I'm twenty-nine years old, and I haven't lived in a cocoon all my life. This isn't the first pass I've had made at me. I was dealing with the situation."

"You didn't look like you were dealing with it very well." He took a long swallow of the whiskey. "Kenyon was all over you, and you weren't exactly screaming for help."

"Of course I wasn't screaming for help! My God, Garth, think of the scene that would have caused. A woman doesn't scream when she finds herself in that sort of mess. She deals with it as an adult. We were at a party and one of the men got drunk and made a pass. I was about to walk away from him when you arrived. It was a very simple if not particularly pleasant situation. It did not require you to order me out of the house and into the car as if I were a misbehaving child."

"Your behavior wasn't exactly childlike, I'll grant you that." He finished the rest of the whiskey while Shannon stared at him in outrage. "Those kinds of games are strictly for grown-ups."

"Garth, stop it. You have no reason to be angry. I wasn't doing anything wrong. For heaven's sake, do you think I deliberately got myself cornered by Kenyon?"

"No."

Shannon closed her eyes briefly in relief. "Well, thanks for that much faith, at any rate."

"I think," Garth continued bluntly, "that you got yourself trapped because you were naive and a little foolish. You don't know this crowd, Shannon. You live in a different world. People such as Kenyon are barracudas. They'll turn on anything that looks like it might be food."

"Damn it, Garth, I am not a silly, naive female. I know about the real world."

"Is that right? Then that only leaves us one other explanation for your behavior, doesn't it?"

Shannon paled. "What are you talking about?"

He crossed his arms over his chest and studied her coolly. "If you didn't get into that clinch with Kenyon because you were too naive to avoid him, then we have to assume you were in it because you were enjoying the situation."

Shannon felt as though everything around her was starting to crack. Desperately she fought to hold on to the fracturing pieces. "Garth, you must know better than that. I would never betray you. I'm not your ex-wife. *I'm not Christine.*"

He went very still, his eyes frozen. When he spoke, the words were chips of ice. "You were very busy tonight, weren't you? Who told you about Christine?"

Belatedly, Shannon wished she had kept her mouth shut. It was too late now. Wearily she replied. "Mrs. Hutchinson mentioned her." There was no need to bring up the fact that Kenyon had also mentioned Christine. Matters were bad enough as it was.

"Ellen Hutchinson never could keep her mouth shut. Did she tell you all the grim details?"

Shannon shook her head in quick denial. "She . . . she only mentioned that you had been married and that there had been a divorce."

"She obviously told you more than that." Garth turned around to pour himself another drink. "Did she mention James Brice?"

Feeling as if she were stepping into a quagmire, Shannon clasped her hands in front of her and answered in a soft voice, "Ellen said Christine had left you to marry someone named James. That was the end of it, Garth. That's all I know. I shouldn't have said anything. It's just that you're making it sound as if I was planning to run off with Kenyon or something, and it was so absurd that I couldn't think of any way to defend myself."

Garth swung around again, pinning her with a savage look. "James Brice was my partner and I thought he was my friend. Christine was my wife. They were having an affair. The situation is as old as the hills, but I didn't even see it coming until it was all over. That was five years ago, Shannon, and I was not exactly a naive innocent myself at the time. I had already built up a successful, highly competitive business, and you don't do that around here unless you're capable of watching your own back while you go after someone else's throat. I had met my share of women who use their bodies as bargaining tools. And I had seen enough friends and partners turn on each other to know you couldn't trust very many people. I thought I was fairly street-wise, but Chris and Jim still managed to take me by surprise. And you tell me you can handle someone like Ed Kenyon? You don't know what the hell you're talking about. Your idea of sophistication is having a couple of friends who have decided to have a baby without getting married and going to feminist performances of *The Taming of the Shrew*. You're a babe in the woods here in my world."

Shannon's eyes widened with sudden realization. "And you're afraid that if I spend too much time in this world, I'll learn my way around in it, aren't you? That's why you don't want me here. You want to keep me safely tucked away on the coast where you can enjoy me on occasional weekends."

"I don't want you mixed up with the kind of people I deal with on a day-to-day basis," Garth said through gritted teeth.

Shannon saw the pain that flashed in his eyes, and all her defensiveness dissolved beneath the overwhelming desire to reassure and comfort him. He had been brutalized by his world, and his instincts had been to keep her out of it. He had been trying to protect her and himself. Shannon smiled tremulously and went forward in a small, soft rush, wrapping her arms tightly around his rigid body. She nestled her head against his shoulder, willing him to relax.

"Garth, I'm not Christine. Please trust me."

He exhaled heavily, enfolding her in a harsh embrace and burying his face in her hair. "It's not a question of trust. I'm only trying to protect you."

"I'm not that fragile. Or that weak." She lifted her head and met his eyes. "And my emotions aren't that superficial. I love you, Garth."

He stared down at her for a long moment, as if a declaration of love had been the last thing he'd expected to hear. Then, with a low groan, he took her mouth.

Shannon made no protest, though the kiss was ruthless in its intensity. She could feel the urgent need for reassurance behind it, and in that moment all she wanted to do was provide what Garth needed.

"Shannon, sweet Shannon," he ground out against her mouth. His hands kneaded her slender back, working their way down to her waist. She could feel the strength of them through the thin silk of her dress.

"I love you, Garth. I love you." Closing her eyes, she clung to him. He was fumbling with the delicate fastenings of the silk now. She didn't care when she heard the faint tearing sound. Garth swore under his breath.

"Damn it to hell, I'm as clumsy as a kid on his first date tonight."

"It's all right." She soothed him, her fingertips working with gentle urgency on the sleek muscles of his shoulders. "I don't care about the dress."

"I'll buy you another one." He pulled the dress down to her waist and then over her hips. It fell into a pool of brightly patterned gold at her feet. "Say it again, Shannon. I want to hear you say it again."

She ran her fingertips through his hair, her eyes brimming with emotion. "I love you, Garth."

The lambent flame of his gaze seemed to be melting all the ice she was accustomed to seeing in his eyes. "Undress me, Shannon. I want to feel your hands all over me."

Obediently she began struggling with the buttons of his white shirt. For some reason it was a difficult task. Garth didn't seem to mind. He toyed with the tendrils of her hair and grazed her nipples with the pad of his thumb while she worked.

The pieces of his clothing fell away in agonizing slowness. By the time she had finished, Shannon was violently aware of her own flaring desire. When at last they both stood naked she ran her hands over the hard contours of his chest.

"I would have missed you so much this weekend," she breathed. "I couldn't stay away."

"Shannon, you don't know what you do to me." He kissed her until she melted against him, and then he slowly sank down to his knees in front of her, his lips finding all the gentle curves and hollows of her body. His fingers tightened on her buttocks as he brushed his mouth across her thigh.

"Garth." His name was a sweet, soft gasp of pleasure and need. "Please, Garth."

"Yes, honey. I'll please you. Come here and let me make love to you." He pulled her down beside him and then tumbled her gently onto the rug. He filled her mouth with his kisses as he luxuriously lowered himself along the length of her body. He was rigid with a need that had flashed into existence with the white-hot rapidity of a forest fire.

Shannon opened herself to him with a feminine honesty that brought Garth to a raging peak of desire. She could feel him fighting to control himself as he drove into her.

"Hold me," he pleaded through clenched teeth. "Hold me, Shannon."

She moaned softly and pulled him to her, her thighs enclosing him as he began the powerful, sensual rhythm. Her teeth sank delicately into his shoulder, and Garth responded with almost violent passion. His own teeth found the sensitive skin of her throat, and he nipped carefully. Shannon's mind swirled with excitement. Within moments she was crying out his name and shivering in his arms. When he lifted his head and saw the dazed discovery in her face, Garth let himself be sucked into the shimmering vortex. Together they hung suspended in space and then, very slowly, returned to a waiting reality.

For long moments Shannon lay beneath Garth's weight, delighting in the feel of him on virtually every inch of her body. Her fingers moved lovingly on his shoulders and at the nape of his neck. For a while she thought he had gone to sleep, then Garth spoke softly.

"I'm sorry I raked you over the coals tonight, Shannon."

"I understand. Did you love her very much?"

"Christine?" He rolled to one side, lying beside Shannon on the gray carpet. He touched the valley between her small breasts, stroking the dampness there in absent wonder. "Christine and I had what seemed like a well-organized and successful marriage. She was beautiful and ambitious. She married me because I was going places, and I married her because I knew she'd look good beside me when I got to those places. We had a lot in common. She had worked in the high-tech world ever since she had graduated, and she was interested in my work. More interested than I realized, as I found out when she and Jim left with several company proprietary designs." Garth put his arm across his eyes. "I guess Jim felt he had a right to those designs. After all, he'd been my partner for two years. What got to me was that they were *my* designs. Ones I had done on my own. I wouldn't have cared so much if he'd just taken company stuff." There was a pause before Garth added, "It was Christine who turned my work over to him. I'd been doing some revisions at home in the evenings, and she knew all about them."

Shannon touched him. "I'm not Christine, Garth."

"I know." He cradled her against him. "I know that, Shannon. I have never mistaken you for her. I couldn't. Not in a million years. I couldn't get you mixed up with any other woman I've ever met. You're unique."

He picked her up and carried her into the bedroom, settling her gently into the wide bed and then he was pulling her close again, whispering words of need and passion and fire. Shannon responded with an answering spiral of emotions that flared to match his own. It was a long while before they slept, their legs tangled together and Shannon nestled safely in Garth's embrace. Shannon was comfortingly aware of Garth's strength just as she closed her eyes. The future would be good, she thought. She would make it work.

IT WAS SHORTLY AFTER DAWN when Shannon first stirred the next morning. She came awake with a vague sense of disorientation and lay quietly for a moment wondering why some element in the atmosphere felt wrong. Garth's bed was a large one, and she couldn't feel his weight beside her. That was a definite change. All night long she had been pleasantly aware of his warmth and reassuring weight lying next to her.

Opening her eyes with sleepy curiosity, she turned over and blinked at the empty space on the other side of the bed. A small frisson of alarm went through her. There was no cause for it, she assured herself. He must be already up and in the shower. But there was no sound of running water from the adjoining bath.

"Garth?"

"I'm right here, Shannon."

The darkness in his voice sent another shiver through her. Panic leaped alive in her veins, consuming the contentment that should have been hers this morning. Something was terribly wrong. Slowly Shannon sat up against the pillows and looked at Garth.

He was sitting in the chair beside the window, dressed in a pair of slacks and a shirt that was only half buttoned. In the morning light his face looked like that of a predator. All the ice she thought she had melted in him last night was back in his eyes. There was a stapled document on the table beside him. It was the only thing cluttering the austere tabletop. Shannon froze, sensing utter disaster and not yet knowing from what direction it would come.

"Garth, what is it? What's wrong?"

Wordlessly he reached out and picked up the document. Tossing it down on the bed beside her, he sat waiting for her to pick it up and read it.

The first thing Shannon saw was the Confidential stamp on the cover. The letters were in black, instead of the original red, which meant she was looking at a photocopy. In the lower right-hand corner the name Sherilectronics was typed in neat capital letters. The company logo was printed beside it. In the center of the cover page were the words "Submitted to Carstairs, Inc." Shannon let the document slip from her fingers as she lifted her eyes to meet Garth's steady, brooding gaze.

"I don't understand," she whispered.

"A few minutes ago I went out into the living room to collect your clothes and your tote bag. When I glanced inside the bag I saw that rolled up and stuffed into a corner. Recognize it?"

Shannon was trembling. "I can read. It's that bid package you've been working on for the past few weeks."

"Months," he corrected calmly. "My company has been working on that proposal for months, not just a few weeks. I want that contract very badly, Shannon."

If only there were some emotion in his voice, Shannon thought frantically. She might have been able to deal with emotion, even if it was fury. But there was nothing, no anger or pain, not even accusation. Shannon's mouth went dry. "I don't understand, Garth."

"Don't you? It seems simple enough to me."

"You think I stole this?" Shannon asked so softly that she could barely hear the words herself.

Garth didn't say anything for a while, and then he got to his feet. "Get dressed and come on out into the living room. I don't think the bedroom is the place for this kind of conversation. Although God knows I didn't do such a clever job of handling you in the living room last night, either."

Shannon came out of her paralysis and reached for his hand as he brushed past the bed. "Garth, wait," she pleaded, "tell me exactly what you think I've done. I have a right to know what the accusation is this time."

"This time?"

"Last night you accused me of letting Ed Kenyon make a pass," she reminded him through tight lips.

He shook off her hand, glanced down at the proposal and continued toward the door. "On the surface this all looks connected, doesn't it? Kenyon is my main opponent in the battle to get the Carstairs contract. Last night he was trying to get you into bed, and this morning I find that copy of the bid package in your purse. It should make for an interesting story. I can't wait to listen to it."

He was gone before Shannon could think of a single word in her own defense. Stunned, she sat looking blindly at the damning document lying amid the tumbled sheets and blankets. *Garth had found this terrible thing in her tote bag.*

It was more than she could handle this time. Numbly Shannon climbed out of bed and stumbled into the bathroom. It was too much. She felt totally overwhelmed. Last night she had been prepared to argue her own case. She was not a coward. She was willing to fight for her love. But this morning the evidence was too awful, and the jury was already prejudiced against her. There would be nothing left for Garth to do except carry out the sentence.

Shannon stood shakily in front of the sink, looking into the reflection of her own eyes. Her stomach was churning and she prayed she wouldn't get sick. She hardly recognized the desolate stranger standing in front of her. All hope had flown from that empty gaze. Her eyes were only mirroring the emptiness in her heart.

"Oh, my dearest love," she whispered, "there's nothing I can say or do this time. It's gone too far. You will never trust me or love me now." Her eyes burned but she couldn't even find the release of tears.

A faint sound from the kitchen reached her, jarring Shannon out of the numb contemplation of her own image. Garth was out there, waiting for the final confrontation. She knew in that moment she couldn't face him. He must hate her.

Through the open bathroom door she saw her tote sitting on the floor beside the dressing table. Her keys would be inside and her little Fiat waited in Garth's driveway. Escape was the only goal now. She had to get out of Garth's house. She couldn't look again into the face of the man she had loved, knowing what he thought she had done.

Shannon fumbled with the shower, turning on the water but not stepping into the stall. As long as the water was running Garth would assume she was in the bathroom. Moving awkwardly at first and then with increasing speed, Shannon dressed from the small suitcase she had brought with her. When she had fastened her jeans, pulled on one of her own silk-screened T-shirts and found her sandals, she picked up her things and headed for the sliding glass door of the bedroom.

A moment later she was letting herself out of the garden through the gate that opened onto the common grounds shared by the condominium owners. Without giving herself a chance to think, she dug her keys out of the tote and raced toward the front of Garth's place. The Fiat was sitting where she had left it yesterday, after following Garth home from Sherilectronics. She was inside, her tote and suitcase tossed behind the seat in a matter of seconds.

Shannon turned the key in the ignition. A moment later she was fleeing out onto the street, racing away from the doom she couldn't face.

Inside the condo, Garth heard the Fiat's engine and realized too late what was happening. He wrenched open the front door in time to see the little red car disappear down the street. He stared after it, his hand curling into a fist as he braced himself in the doorway.

"Damn you, Shannon. You weren't supposed to run."

THE TRIP BACK UP THE COAST seemed endless. At one point Shannon grimly pointed out to herself that the long drive would have eventually come between herself and Garth, even if she'd played the meek little mistress and stayed on the coast. How many weekends would a man want to drive this far just to go to bed with a woman? There were women living much more conveniently near San Jose.

By the time she turned off Highway 101 and found the narrow two-lane road that led toward home,

Shannon thought she had come to terms with the situation.

She had made a terrible mistake the day she had first approached Garth Sheridan. In his own way he had tried to tell her that much. She had to give him credit. He hadn't exactly encouraged her in the beginning. It was as if, deep down, he knew his own emotional limitations.

But she had been so sure of herself. So sure of him. From the first she had wanted to know what made Garth tick. She had kept pushing until she had gotten past his very private, very personal barriers. Now she was paying the price for her compulsion.

The fog was rolling in lazily off the ocean as Shannon finally pulled into the safety of her own driveway. She turned off the engine and leaned wearily against the steering wheel, staring at her front door. After a moment she opened the car door and climbed stiffly out. It had been a very long drive.

The phone was ringing as she carried her suitcase and tote inside the cottage. For an instant she considered not answering it. She knew who would be on the other end of the line. On the fourth ring she reluctantly picked up the receiver.

"Hello."

Garth's voice came across the line, harsh and cold. "I just wanted to make sure you got home safely."

"You don't have to worry about me anymore, Garth. I'm a big-time industrial spy, remember? I can take care of myself."

"Damn it, Shannon, listen to me...."

She put down the receiver very softly and unplugged the phone. It was as she sat staring at her tote bag that the tears finally came. It was a relief to give in to them at last.

SHANNON GOT UP EARLY the next morning to take the first crib stencil designs to Annie O'Connor. The other woman greeted her cheerfully at the door of the comfortable, weathered old house she shared with Dan Turcott.

"Come on in. I just took a whole-grain coffee cake out of the oven. Want a slice?" Annie stood aside.

"Sounds great. Here are the stencil designs. See what you think."

Annie tore open the packet as she led the way into the rustic kitchen that was redolent with fresh, warm, yeasty smells. "Oh, Shannon, they're wonderful. The baby's going to love them!"

Shannon managed a small smile at the comment. "How are you feeling, Annie?"

The other woman stretched and idly massaged her lower back. "Great. I feel as if I'm finally doing what I was meant to do."

"Have babies?" Shannon grinned faintly.

"Go ahead and laugh. I'm going to make a terrific mother." Annie began cutting up the hot coffee cake.

"I believe you. I think Dan's going to make a good father, too."

Annie carried the plates over to the table and sat down. "He's asked me to marry him, you know," she said quietly.

Shannon looked at her in astonishment. "No, I didn't know. I thought you two were determined to do this your own way."

Annie shrugged. "I was. I thought Dan was, too. But the other day he sat down at breakfast and told me he thought we should get married. You know what I think? I think it was something your friend Garth said at dinner that night. Dan is starting to talk about providing me and the baby with the protection of his name. How's that for old-fashioned gallantry?"

"I'm stunned."

"Yeah. So was I, considering the kind of books he writes," Annie admitted with a smile. "But I think I'll take him up on it."

"You're going to get married?"

Annie nodded thoughtfully. "With the baby on the way, I'm ready for the commitment. So is Dan. You'll have to be sure and bring Garth to the wedding."

Shannon took a bite of coffee cake, hardly tasting it. "That's not very likely."

"The weekend was a disaster?"

"To put it mildly. He never wanted me to go to San Jose in the first place. I thought I'd surprise him. As it turns out, I did. Before I went he assumed I was a naive, impulsive, artsy-craftsy type who would make an ideal, uncomplicated, undemanding weekend mistress. Not real bright, but warm and willing, and he wouldn't have to worry about me causing him any real trouble."

Annie slowly poured coffee and added cream. "And now?"

"Now he thinks I'm a slick corporate spy who sells her body and her secrets to the highest bidder."

Annie stared at her friend, her eyes full of astonishment. "Quite a change in perception in one weekend," she remarked dryly. "Want to tell me about it?"

Over warm coffee cake and creamy coffee, Shannon did. When she was finished she didn't feel much better, but she knew she had reached a degree of acceptance. She went back home and back to work.

It wasn't until the next day that Shannon remembered the buyer's contract she had been holding to show to Garth. She dug it out of the tote bag where she had put it to take with her to San Jose and quickly scanned the fine print. The contract looked okay to her. Garth had been right. She didn't completely understand all the whereases and wherefores. No one but a lawyer would, and she didn't feel like locating a lawyer. No point waiting any longer to sign. In her present mood she didn't really care what she signed. She picked up her pen and was about to start her signature on the bottom line when she heard the Porsche in the drive.

For an instant panic assailed her. She glanced quickly around the cottage as if seeking a hiding place. The forceful knock on the door brought her to her feet.

"Damn you, Garth Sheridan," she muttered under her breath. "This is my home and I'm on my territory. I'm not going to let you terrorize me here." Angrily she walked across the room and flung open the door.

"Well?" she demanded as he stood looking down at her with brooding eyes. "Have you come to arrest me?"

"Not exactly. Invite me in, Shannon. I've come to ask you to marry me."

7

SHANNON WAS SO NONPLUSSED that she could only
stand and stare at the man on her threshold. It took a
supreme effort of will to gather her senses. "If this is
your idea of a joke, Garth, it borders on sick."

"You know me better than that, Shannon. I rarely
make jokes, sick or otherwise. I do, however, occasionally make mistakes. Please let me inside."

"Mistakes?" she demanded sharply. In spite of her
intentions, something about the expression in his eyes
made her stand aside. "Garth, what are you talking
about? Why have you driven all this way? Don't you
have to be back in your precious Sherilectronics office bright and early tomorrow morning?"

He moved past her, planting himself solidly in the
room. Slowly he turned to face Shannon, his eyes
gentling. "Close the door, honey. We have to talk."

"I don't think I want to hear what you have to say,
Garth." Reluctantly she closed the door and stood
waiting, one hand still on the knob as if she were contemplating a mad dash to freedom. The notion irritated her. This was her house, Shannon reminded
herself. She wasn't about to let Garth Sheridan drive
her from it.

"I know you're upset, Shannon. You shouldn't have panicked and run Sunday morning. You never gave me a chance to explain."

"What was there to explain?" she challenged hotly. "You found all the evidence you needed to try and convict me. You can't blame me if I didn't hang around for the sentencing. Any self-respecting prisoner would run if she got the chance. Did you expect me to sit humbly on your living room sofa while you delivered judgment?"

"Calm down, Shannon." He walked into her kitchen and opened a cupboard door. The bottle of whiskey he had left with her was still inside. Garth poured himself a glass, his face set in hard, weary lines. "It's obvious you're still on edge. You shouldn't have gotten behind the wheel of a car Sunday morning feeling as upset as you did. It's not safe to drive when your mood is unstable."

"I can't believe this! You're standing there in my kitchen giving me safety lectures? At a time like this?"

His mouth twisted in a wry grimace as he leaned back against the counter and took a sip of the whiskey. "Force of habit. Or maybe I'm trying to figure out how to get back to the main subject."

"What is the main subject?"

"I told you. Marriage." His eyes met hers with steady intent.

She shook her head in incomprehension. "I don't understand what you're talking about, Garth."

"Sit down," he said gently. "I'll explain it to you." He came toward her, put a hand on her arm and led her back out into the living room. Very carefully he seated her on the sofa and then he took the comfortable overstuffed chair near the fireplace. "Relax, Shannon. Please. God knows I'm tense enough for both of us."

"Then you shouldn't have gotten behind the wheel of a car and driven a couple of hundred miles."

He raised his eyebrows. "That was childish."

"I know," she agreed sadly.

"I drove two hundred miles because I had to talk to you. You didn't hang around Sunday morning long enough to discuss the matter, and Sunday night you hung up on me. I got the impression you'd do it again if I called."

"Probably. I have no desire to talk to a man who thinks I'm a corporate spy."

"I don't think you're a corporate spy, Shannon."

She stared at him. "That's not the impression I got Sunday morning."

"Sunday morning I had a lot of thinking to do." Garth looked down into his whiskey. "It was a shock."

"Finding that damn proposal in my tote? Yes," she said bitterly, "I imagine it was. It was a shock to me, too. But I don't expect you to believe that."

"I believe it."

Shannon's head came around with a snap, her eyes troubled and wary. "You do?"

"I don't believe you stole that proposal, Shannon."

"But on Sunday you acted as if you'd just discovered I was Mata Hari."

"I couldn't figure out what was going on," he said quietly. "I wanted some answers. Instead of giving them to me, you ran."

"What did you expect me to do?"

"Given your impulsive, temperamental approach to things, I guess I should have expected you to do exactly what you did."

She gritted her teeth over the "impulsive" and "temperamental." "What conclusion did you come to on your own?"

"The obvious one. You were used."

"Used? How was I used? What are you talking about?"

"Shannon, it's pretty clear you just happened to be in the wrong place at the wrong time." Garth sat forward, his elbows on his knees, glass held lightly in both hands as he talked intently. "I don't know what was supposed to be going on in that bedroom at the Hutchinsons' party, but it looks like someone was using it to pass that copy of the bid proposal to a, shall we say, interested party."

"Kenyon?"

"Who knows? The information in that bid package would have been interesting to several other people who were there that night, not just Kenyon. We may never know. Whoever was trying to make the transfer is hardly likely to come forward now and claim the document got lost."

Shannon chewed thoughtfully on her lower lip. "Let me get this straight. You're saying someone used my tote to hide the copy of the bid proposal while waiting to make his deal?"

Garth nodded. "It's a possibility. A reasonable explanation."

"And it was just my bad luck whoever it was used my tote?"

"Your bag was very distinctive. Easy to spot among a pile of purses. Easy to describe to the person who was supposed to collect the document. Shannon, this is purely speculation on my part. But it's the best I can come up with at the moment. As I said, it doesn't really matter now. The proposal got intercepted."

"Thanks to me," she couldn't resist pointing out. "Maybe you owe me something for that, Garth. Have you looked at the matter from that angle?"

Garth raised his eyebrows but didn't comment on that. "Shannon, I didn't want you getting involved with the business side of my life. I wanted to keep you clear of it." He swore in soft disgust. "But even I couldn't have guessed it would get as messy as it did the first time you showed up in San Jose."

Shannon couldn't ignore the pain in his voice. She felt her resolve weakening. "It was pure bad luck. You said it yourself. I was in the wrong place at the wrong time." She hesitated and then asked cautiously, "So you drove all this way to apologize?"

"I told you why I drove all this way. I'm here to ask you to marry me."

She clasped her hands together tightly in her lap, aware that her pulse was suddenly racing. "But, Garth, why?"

"You love me," he said quietly. "You said so. We're good together, you and I. We have something unique. If we're married I'll be in a better position to take care of you. I won't have to worry so much about your impulsiveness. And I think that once we're married you'll be a lot less likely to run whenever we find ourselves confronting a problem. You'll stay and face the issue."

"What makes you so certain?" Shannon asked tightly.

He frowned, obviously sorting through his words. "Marriage will put restraints on your behavior, Shannon. You'll be more inclined to listen to me. I think you'll be a lot more likely to accept my protection."

"Protection? You're making it sound as if you're going to be my jailer, not my husband!"

He groaned. "I don't mean it that way and I think you know it. Shannon, I want to take care of you. I want to know you're following my advice. I want to keep you out of the kind of situation you got into the other night at that party."

Shannon's emotions were so jumbled that she could hardly breathe. "You think that if we're married I'm going to be more inclined to be meek and obedient?"

"I think," he said softly, "that if we're married, you'll be more reasonable about some things."

"Less likely to play spy, for example?" she got out through clenched teeth.

"I've already told you I don't believe you were playing corporate spy the other night."

For some reason the deliberately soothing tone of his voice enraged her. Shannon realized she was trembling with the force of her reaction. It was ludicrous. Here she was receiving a proposal of marriage from the man she loved, and all she wanted to do was hurl it back in his face because she was getting it for all the wrong reasons. "You want to marry me because you've decided you want to go on sleeping with me and you think you'll find our weekend affair more comfortable if you have more control over me. Does that about sum it up, Garth? Have I got all the facts straight?"

"I'm not talking about controlling you, damn it, I'm talking about protecting you."

"It's a matter of opinion."

The whiskey glass came down on the end table with a violent crash as Garth surged to his feet. Shoving his hands into his pockets in a gesture that made his tension plain, he stalked to the far end of the small, cozy room and turned to glare at her. "Shannon, I am not blaming you for what happened the other night. I'm blaming myself. I shouldn't have allowed you to be put into a position where you could get used the way you were used. I want to protect you. I want to keep you out of that side of my life. I don't want you get-

ting sucked into the back-stabbing and the politics of
my world. You're not cut out for it."

"You mean I'm too dumb and naive to survive in it,
don't you? I'll tell you something, Garth. I don't know
which I prefer least—having you think I'm a corporate spy or having you think I'm too naive to be one.
Neither is a compliment to me. You've got a hell of a
lot of nerve showing up on my doorstep tonight saying you want to marry me, when all you really want
to do is keep this affair of ours running on your terms.
It's yourself you're trying to protect, Garth, not me.
You think that if I'm wearing your ring I'll be easier to
manage, less of an unknown quantity. You'll feel more
in command, won't you?"

"Shannon, you're twisting my words. Now just
calm down and think about this logically for a few
minutes."

"I can't think logically. I'm an artist, remember? I'm
temperamental, volatile and unpredictable. And I'll
tell you something else, Garth, that much isn't going
to change if I marry you. I'll still be just as temperamental, volatile and unpredictable. It's in the blood!"

"You're angry."

"Brilliant observation. I'm downright furious."

"Let me take you out to dinner. It will give you a
chance to calm down," he suggested quietly.

"I don't want a chance to calm down!"

"Shannon, listen to me—"

"No, you listen to me," she shot back. "It's been
hard enough trying to adjust to the idea of being your

weekend mistress. I'll be damned if I'll play the role of weekend wife. You're right about one thing—I am a lot freer with things the way they have been. But I'll be freer still when I stop being available to you entirely."

He started toward her. "Shannon, you're all wound up. Calm down and give yourself some time to get accustomed to the idea. Don't say a lot of things you'll regret later."

"I won't regret any of this. The only things I do regret are the weekends I've already thrown away on you!"

"We've both had some adjusting to do—"

She didn't allow him to finish. "You haven't done any adjusting at all that I can see. I'm the only one who's been expected to adjust and that is coming to a halt right now. Go back to San Jose and your backstabbing friends, Garth. I'm not in the market for a weekend husband or even a weekend lover."

His eyes glittered with a repressed fury that seemed to have sprung up out of nowhere. Shannon took an uncertain step backward, startled at the lightning change in his mood. Until now he had been frustratingly and infuriatingly calm. All of a sudden Shannon had the feeling she was facing a barely leashed storm.

"You love me." It was a statement, not a plea or a guess.

"Weekend lovers can fall out of love as quickly as they fall into it. It doesn't take much to ruin the mood. Just one lousy weekend!"

"Stop it, Shannon."

"I don't want you in my life," she flung back, goaded. "You're too hard and ruthless for my world. You're not cut out for it."

"You should have figured that out before you cornered me on the beach that first morning," he rasped. Then he was in front of her, crowding her against the wall and cutting off her escape. "Shannon, you can't walk away from what we have. Not now. It's much too late."

His mouth came down on hers, his arms going around her to lock her to him. Shannon gasped beneath the onslaught of his kiss, prepared to struggle with all her strength. But the moment his lips met hers, the fight went out of her. The hunger in him was as strong as ever, but now there was a kind of masculine desperation underlying the embrace. She sensed the need in him and knew with feminine intuition that it was far more than physical.

Garth's emotions ran deep. She had known that on some level the first morning she had approached him. A part of her had been convinced even then that he had the soul of a poet. The dark, brooding quality hadn't changed, not even when she had discovered him to be from the business world instead of the literary or artistic world. The compulsion she had felt to know him completely was as strong as ever in her,

Shannon discovered. And the need to love him and quiet the dark tension in him was just as fierce.

"Garth..."

"Shannon, I don't want to be at war with you. I only want to take you in my arms and keep you safe. Love me, don't fight me." His mouth moved intimately on hers, seeking the reassurance of a response.

Shannon found herself struggling against both her own instincts and Garth's sensual pleasure. She tore her mouth free from his and braced her palms on his shoulders. "Not like this," she whispered. "You can't walk in here and put everything back the way it was by taking me to bed."

"I don't want things back the way they were. I want you to marry me." He framed her face with his large hands.

Shannon caught her breath and grabbed at the only lifeline she could see. "Dinner. You said you'd take me out to dinner."

His eyes narrowed for a moment. Then, with obvious reluctance, his hands fell away. "All right. Anything rather than have you throw me out the door."

Shannon realized her hands were shaking as she came away from the wall.

TELLING HIMSELF HE MUST BE satisfied with the small victory he had achieved, Garth treated Shannon with kid gloves for the rest of the evening. It was crazy to be feeling so relieved, but he was convinced he'd had a very near miss. He hadn't expected her to be so totally resistant to the idea of marrying him. Her reaction had taken him by surprise. He had convinced himself that she would be reassured by the proposal and instead found out that he was the one in need of reassurance.

It had all seemed so simple during the long drive from San Jose. He would tell Shannon that he had never really suspected her of corporate espionage, that somehow, someone had used her. It was the truth. When he'd seen that bid package fall out of her tote bag, he'd been stunned, but even in that moment he couldn't bring himself to believe his sweet Shannon was betraying him. The whole sorry mess would serve to illustrate exactly why he wanted her kept clear of his steel-trapped environment. She needed his protection, and he needed to know she was safe. On the surface, the proposal of marriage seemed logical and would provide reassurance for both of them.

But he hadn't realized just how deep her temperamental streak of independence went, Garth thought as he drove Shannon the short distance into town. Still, by morning everything should be back under control. When she was in his arms she melted completely. The last of her indignation and fear would be gone by morning. He'd see to it.

The small restaurant was located in an old farmhouse, and it was run by friends of Shannon's. The food was an interesting mix of traditional Creole cooking and nouvelle California cuisine. Garth made sure Shannon's wineglass was full during the meal. He decided he wasn't too proud to make use of the traditional soothing effect of alcohol on a woman. Hell, tonight he wasn't too proud to use any technique he could to lure Shannon back into his arms.

She didn't talk much during dinner, and Garth suspected that what little she did say was more to keep her friends from wondering about her mood than because she wanted to communicate with him. Most of the time she seemed lost in thought. As the meal progressed Garth realized he'd give a great deal to be able to read her mind.

Shannon had declined the pecan pie and was polishing off the last of the corn bread when a familiar greeting caused her to glance up. Garth looked up, too, and saw Annie O'Connor and Dan Turcott being seated at the table next to them.

"Hi, Shannon, Garth." Annie nodded pleasantly as Dan seated her. "What are you doing up here in the middle of the week, Garth? Shannon tells me you're only free on weekends."

"I made an exception this week." He knew he sounded forbidding, but he couldn't help it. Garth didn't feel like socializing tonight.

"Maybe it was fate," Dan said with a grin. "You can help us celebrate. Annie and I are getting married soon."

Garth eyed the other couple. "Congratulations."

"Isn't it great, Garth?" Shannon asked with suspicious blandness. "We just knew you'd approve."

He felt uncomfortable, convinced he was being set up and not sure how to handle it. There was a dangerous glitter in Shannon's eyes. "I do approve," he said simply. "As a matter of fact, I've just asked Shannon to marry me."

"That's wonderful!" Annie's eyes went quickly from Garth's face to that of her friend and then she reached over to hug a stiff Shannon. "The end of the weekend affair, Shannon," she murmured.

"Not quite," Shannon said loudly enough for everyone nearby to hear. "Garth's thinking of substituting a weekend marriage for the affair."

There was an embarrassed hush during which Garth was shocked to realize that he was flushing. A woman hadn't succeeded in embarrassing him this much since he was fourteen years old. In that moment he could cheerfully have bound and gagged Shannon and carried her bodily out of the restaurant. Annie O'Connor grinned knowingly.

"A weekend marriage will never work, Garth. You'll have to make some major modifications in your life-style, I'm afraid. Marriage is a very serious matter. It's not something you can conduct on the weekends. What good is a weekend husband?"

Garth knew he had just been repaid for the comments he had made that first night he'd been invited to dinner at Shannon's cottage. A sense of fair play made him acknowledge Annie's victory. "You have a point, Annie. I'll have to think about it. If you've finished gnawing on that corn bread, Shannon, we can be on our way." He paid the check without waiting to see if she was going to come along willingly. Sometimes you had to assume obedience in order to get it. It was a risk, but under the circumstances Garth couldn't think of anything else to do. He wanted to take Shannon home and make love to her. He definitely did not want to sit here and let her use Annie's and Dan's presence to bait him.

Garth got to his feet, hiding his inner fear that Shannon might simply continue to sit and chat with Annie and ignore him altogether. To his relief she reluctantly stood and said her good-nights. Garth hastened her out of the restaurant and into the waiting Porsche.

"That fog is rolling in late tonight," he said, trying for a neutral note in the conversation as he started the car. When he switched on the headlights the beams bounced back off a misty, swirling bank of fog. He lowered them and slowly edged the Porsche out onto the narrow road that would take them back to the cottage.

"Where are you going to stay, Garth?" Shannon asked calmly.

The question threw him. "Are you going to fight me down to the wire, honey?"

"That depends. Are you attacking?"

His fingers tightened on the wheel. "What do you think?"

She sighed and slumped back against the seat. "I don't know what to think Garth. I need some time."

"I'll give you time."

"Will you?"

The skepticism in her voice annoyed him. "You sound as if you don't trust me, Shannon. What have I ever done to make you distrust me?"

There was a short silence from the other seat. "Nothing," Shannon said at last. "You've been very honest with me right from the start."

"I'll always be honest with you, Shannon."

"I believe you."

"Then trust me enough to let me stay with you tonight," he urged. He didn't dare let her send him away, Garth thought. The situation was too fragile. It would be so easy for her to convince herself that she was better off without him. There was still too much uncertainty and wariness in her. Garth could feel the tangled, volatile emotions radiating from her.

"You can stay the night, Garth, mainly because I doubt if you'll be able to find a motel room at this hour without driving several miles. God knows you shouldn't be traveling far in this pea soup."

Garth sucked in his breath, hoping she didn't hear the relief in his voice. "You see how easy it is to slip into a protective role, Shannon? Now you're doing it yourself."

"I'm not being protective, I'm being practical. By the way, if you do stay the night, you'll have to use the spare bed in my studio."

He heard the determination in her voice and stifled a short, blunt curse. "Anything you say, honey." One step at a time, Garth told himself. It was clearly going to take a while to lure her back into the protection of his arms, but he could do it. She loved him, he thought. All she needed was a little time to remember that fact.

Sometimes, Garth knew, it took a while to get things into perspective. He had been learning that lesson himself during the past year. Slowly but surely during the past few months he had been coming to terms with some of the dissatisfaction and restlessness he had been feeling for a long time. He still hadn't reached all the conclusions but he knew that deep within himself he was getting ready to alter his life.

The only problem had been that, although he sensed he needed to make a change, there had been no clear alternatives. He had been running Sherilectronics on automatic pilot for a while and he knew it. That knowledge had been one of the reasons he'd decided to go after the Carstairs bid with such relentless effort. It was as if he had to prove to himself that he wasn't really relaxing his grip on his company or his way of life. He could still compete with the best of the Silicon jungle predators and he could still win. Getting the Carstairs contract would prove it.

The trouble was, Garth wasn't certain what he would do after he had won the contract.

SHE COULDN'T SLEEP. Shannon tossed and turned on her bed and tried to will herself into unconsciousness. The harder she worked at it, the more elusive sleep became. She caught herself trying to listen for sounds from the next room, but there were none. Apparently Garth wasn't having the same problem she was. For some reason that irritated her.

Everything annoyed her tonight. She was feeling frustrated, angry and apprehensive. The last thing she had expected was Garth showing up on her doorstep suggesting marriage. It seemed to have sent her into a tailspin.

Giving up on trying to get to sleep, Shannon kicked aside the covers and slid her feet into a pair of slippers. Dressed in only her soft flannel nightgown, she went to the door of her room and opened it. There was no sound in the hall and no sign of light under Garth's door. She slipped out of her room and started silently toward the kitchen. A medicinal shot of Garth's whiskey might be what she needed.

The whiskey bottle clinked slightly against the glass as she poured, but there was no sound from the hall, so Shannon decided Garth hadn't been awakened. Picking up the glass, she went into the living room and sat down to sip the potent whiskey. She curled her feet under her and thought about how out of control her life seemed tonight. It had been a long time since she had felt this off balance, and it was all Garth's fault. Perhaps it all would have worked if only he'd been the brooding poet her imagination had insisted he was. Morosely Shannon contemplated the cruel workings of fate and her own impulsiveness. She wasn't sure which was more depressing.

Sometime later she realized the whiskey wasn't lulling her to sleep. Instead it seemed to have set her mind into a chaotic spin. She found herself silently asking questions for which there were no answers. But above the morass of uncertainties, two things seemed suddenly clear. She would not be able to throw Garth out of her life, and she would not marry a man who saw marriage merely as a way of protecting her and himself. The only answer was to continue the weekend affair.

"Mind if I join you?"

Shannon turned her head at the sound of Garth's voice and saw him standing in the shadows. He was barefoot, wearing only the pants he'd had on earlier. His bare shoulders gleamed briefly in the vague light as he went into the kitchen and collected the whiskey bottle and a glass.

"Did I wake you?" Shannon asked uncertainly as he sat down across from her and poured himself a shot.

"No. I haven't been to sleep. Did you decide to come out here and get drunk by yourself?"

"I've heard it's an effective therapy under certain circumstances," she muttered.

"I tried it Sunday night in San Jose after you made it clear you weren't going to answer your phone. It didn't work very well. The effect is quite temporary." Garth put his feet up on the old leather hassock and took a swallow.

"You got drunk Sunday night because of me?" She couldn't imagine Garth that out of control.

"The memory is vague now, but as I recall I just quietly went unconscious. I took a lot of aspirin the next morning."

"At what point did you decide to ask me to marry you?" she couldn't resist asking. "Sunday night or Monday morning?"

"I'm not going to answer that," he informed her. "It's a loaded question."

They sat sipping from their glasses in silence for a long time after that. Neither tried to force a conversation. For some reason the whiskey and the darkness made it easy to stay curled up in her chair. Shannon began to relax. At last she spoke tentatively.

"I've made a decision, Garth."

He waited, saying nothing.

"I'm willing to try continuing the affair. For a while."

He nodded, as if he'd guessed what she was going to say. "It's better than nothing. I'll take what I can get."

She frowned in the darkness. "It will have to be an affair conducted on my terms, Garth. Do you understand?"

"Yes."

Her mind began to settle as she heard his quiet agreement. Some of the chaos she had been trying to deal with simmered down to a more manageable mixture of doubts and confusion. "I don't know if it's going to work, Garth."

"I'll make it work." There was pure, unadulterated steel underlying the promise. Then there was more silence from him. "I've never deliberately gotten drunk with a woman. It's an interesting experience."

Shannon tilted her head. "Better than drinking alone?"

"Better than sleeping alone."

"Oh." She shut up, thinking about it.

"Is the decision to continue the affair the only thing you've been contemplating out here?" Garth asked after a moment, helping himself to more whiskey and pouring another shot into Shannon's glass.

"Actually, now that you mention it, one other thing did cross my mind," she said carefully.

"What's that?"

"You said something about having a theory that someone used my tote bag that night at the party because it was so vivid and obvious. An easy reference point for a spy wishing to pass along a stolen document."

"It's just a theory."

Shannon nodded. "Not a bad one, though. I can see it now—the thief tells the would-be purchaser of the document where he's hidden the proposal and later, when no one's looking, the purchaser walks casually into the bedroom and removes it from the tote. Very simple."

"And no one observes the thief or his client exchanging anything or looking suspicious," Garth concluded.

"There's just one thing . . ."

"What's that?"

"There were two tote bags lying on that bed the night of the party. Mine and the one I gave Bonnie. What if someone made a mistake and slipped the document into the wrong tote?"

"That," said Garth slowly, "would put a very interesting twist on the situation."

8

IT WAS THE QUIET WAY Garth responded to her question that alarmed Shannon. Trying unsuccessfully to read his face in the shadows, she said quickly, "I didn't mean to imply Bonnie was involved."

"Anything's possible."

"But, Garth, how long has she been working for you?"

"About five years."

"You can't possibly suspect her, then. Surely she's proven herself by now. She's your personal secretary."

Garth was contemplating the label on the bottle of whiskey. "Loyalty is an easily purchased commodity. It can be sold just as easily."

"Maybe it is in your view of the world, but that doesn't mean everyone values it so cheaply," Shannon argued in a despairing tone. She was beginning to realize just how deeply cynical Garth really was. It was frightening. "Besides, I like Bonnie."

Garth shrugged. "She's been a good secretary."

"Don't speak of her as if she's got one foot out the door, damn it. You have no idea whether she's involved in the theft of that stupid bid proposal. I only pointed out the fact that there were two tote bags on the bed Saturday night because I just happened to remember that Bonnie brought one, too. If you're going to suspect anyone, it should still be me. I'm the one you caught with the evidence still in her possession."

Garth slanted her a speculative glance. "You hardly know Bonnie. There's no need to jump to her defense. I haven't accused her of anything yet."

"Well, take my advice and don't make any accusations. If you make her feel she's under suspicion she'll probably quit on the spot. I know I would."

Garth's mouth curved faintly in wry amusement. "You did."

"That's right, I did, didn't I?" Shannon closed her eyes briefly. "Why didn't you let me go, Garth? Why come chasing after me? I can't prove I had nothing to do with that proposal being in my tote. I've got less of an alibi than Bonnie probably has."

"That's not exactly true," Garth said. "Until a few weeks ago you didn't even know me, let alone anything about my business. And last weekend was the first time you'd been to my office or met any of my staff or business associates. Unless everything you've done so far, including introducing yourself on the beach that first time, is part of a very complicated setup, it's highly unlikely you're involved in the theft."

Shannon lifted her lashes and took another sip from her glass. "And I don't look bright enough or sophisticated enough to have arranged a very complicated setup?"

"Shannon . . ."

"No, that's all right, Garth. I don't want to hear any more of your logic. It's not very good for the ego to know that someone thinks you might be innocent by reason of naiveté. But what if it was all part of a very subtle plot concocted by me?" she mused. "Perhaps Ed Kenyon hired me a couple of months ago to get close to you. Perhaps I rented this cottage and set up the silk-screen work just to give myself a cover as soon as I found out you'd rented the cottage next door. I can see it all now, Garth. The beautiful complexity of it boggles the mind. Annie and Dan would have had to be in on it, too, of course. And I might have had to bribe Bonnie. Then there was that clever business with the totes the night of the party. My God, if you look at it that way, I'm a genius."

"If you look at it that way, I'm a complete idiot."

"Well, you wouldn't come off looking like the smartest sort of high-tech executive," she agreed.

He leaned forward, capturing her chin in his hand. In the shadows his eyes gleamed. "Well? Am I a complete idiot? Was this all a giant setup? Am I the fly caught in a web that's so intricate I can't even see the outlines of it?"

"What do you think?" Shannon asked breathlessly.

"I think," Garth said, "that if this really is an involved plot you've concocted, I'm out of my league. I might as well give up now." He brushed his mouth against hers, his kiss warm and persuasive.

"But you don't believe me, do you?"

"No," he admitted, not releasing her. "I think I have only myself to blame for letting you get too close to a world you know nothing about and aren't equipped to handle. You got used by someone in that world and it's my fault. I didn't do a good enough job of protecting you."

"Who is it you want to protect, Garth? Me or yourself?"

"I think, in the end, it amounts to the same thing," he said.

"You want a woman with whom you can relax. Someone who can provide you with a temporary weekend escape from your business and all that."

He smiled a little. "Is that so bad?"

"It's not enough. Not for me."

"I'm offering marriage, Shannon. That should reassure you."

"It's still not enough," she whispered.

"You're fighting both of us, Shannon. It's not just me you're struggling against, it's yourself. You love me, remember?"

"But you don't love me or you wouldn't be offering just a weekend marriage." Very deliberately Shannon put down her glass and got to her feet. "I think I've had enough to drink, Garth. Good night."

He made no move to stop her as she brushed past him and went down the hall to her bedroom. Garth waited until he heard her door close and then he poured a little more whiskey into his glass.

He would give her time. That's what she needed. She'd had an unsettling experience last weekend, and he could hardly blame her for reacting the way she had. She was an artist, he reminded himself. Artists were known for their temperamental behavior. So were women, come to that. The combination of the two was probably dynamite.

Marriage would have been his first choice. He'd reached that decision on Sunday while he'd wandered aimlessly around his home, trying to put together the pieces of the puzzle. But if all he could get from Shannon now was a continuation of the affair, he'd settle for that temporarily. He hadn't been joking when he'd told her he'd take what he could get. He needed Shannon, and he was only now beginning to realize just how much.

Garth finished the last of the whiskey and sat contemplating the darkness. A man had to fight for what he wanted in life. It seemed there was always someone waiting to steal the prize. He'd learned that the hard way. But Garth was accustomed to the battle. He'd fight for Shannon.

THE SMELL OF COFFEE brought Shannon out of a troubled sleep the next morning. She lay still for a moment wondering why she should be able to smell coffee from her own kitchen when she hadn't yet gotten out of bed to make it. Then memory flooded back. She pushed aside the covers and grimly headed for the bathroom.

Half an hour later, dressed in jeans and a button-down shirt, she walked into her kitchen, prepared to dig in her heels again if Garth began talking about marriage. She might be naive and not too bright in some ways, but she could be stubborn when she chose. Every woman had some strong points, she told herself.

"Good morning, Garth." She didn't pause as she headed toward the stove to pour the coffee. "Did you finally get to sleep last night?"

He leaned back in the kitchen chair and nodded a slow greeting. "I got a little."

"You look dressed for the office." Critically she scanned his white shirt and slacks. "Going back early today?"

"I have to leave right after breakfast."

"I'm not surprised. You really shouldn't have wasted the trip yesterday."

He let that pass. "I'll be back on Friday."

"Ah, yes. The weekend."

Garth eyed her speculatively. "You're in a lousy mood this morning, do you know that?"

"Temperamental. Artists are very temperamental."

"Correction. 'Frustrated' is the word that describes you this morning," he said blandly. "You're fighting a losing battle, and you know it." Before she could respond he picked up some papers lying beside him on the table. "I see you at least had the sense to wait and talk to me before you signed this."

Shannon frowned, realizing he was holding the contract the San Francisco buyer had left. "I was just about to sign it yesterday when you arrived."

"I went over it this morning while you were in the shower."

"Garth, I never asked you to vet that contract. You had no business examining it. Here, let me have it."

"Going to sign it as it stands?" he asked.

Suspicious of the neutral tone of his voice, Shannon jerked the contract from his hand. "I don't see any reason why I shouldn't."

"How about the fact that by signing it you'll be agreeing to give that boutique exclusive rights to sell not only your totes but anything else you design for the next six months? They're guaranteeing themselves first right of refusal on all your designs."

"What?" Startled, Shannon scanned the fine print. "I never agreed to anything like that."

"Take a look at clause six."

She read it hurriedly, trying to sort through the jumble of legalese. "Oh, my God," she muttered in disgust. "I read it in a hurry yesterday. I didn't realize . . . I never intended to give the boutique exclusive rights to my products. It's a mistake. I'll have to cross out that clause before I can sign this thing."

"You do that." Garth got up to help himself to more coffee. He stood at the stove, watching Shannon glare at the papers in her hands.

"I don't understand," Shannon tossed the contract back onto the table. "That buyer never said anything about exclusivity."

"Never trust someone who's trying to shove a contract down your throat," Garth advised easily.

"I suppose this is all second nature to you. You're so damn accustomed to people trying to outmaneuver you or cheat you or steal from you." Shannon stalked to the window and stood with her hands on her hips, staring out to sea.

"The buyer wasn't trying to cheat you. She was simply trying to ensure she got the best possible deal for herself."

"Well, she can forget the whole thing. I'm not going to sign that contract, after all."

Garth shook his head. "There's no need to get self-righteous about the situation. Just cross out that clause, sign it and send it back. If she wants those totes, she'll sign it, too, and you'll have a deal. Other than that single clause, it looks like a good contract."

"It's the idea of the thing!"

"It's business."

She spun around. "Honestly, Garth, you're so damn cynical."

He smiled. "Maybe that's why I need you."

She faltered, unsure of how to respond. "I suppose I should thank you for catching that clause."

He moved close and kissed her forehead. "No thanks are necessary. All part of the service."

"The *weekend* service?" she shot back and immediately wished she'd resisted the retort.

"Are you going to be this prickly every weekend?"

Flushing, Shannon turned back to the window. "I don't know. Maybe. Will you lose interest if I am?"

"What do you think?" he asked gently.

"I don't know what to think."

"Well, you'll have plenty of time to consider the matter before I get back on Friday." He didn't sound concerned.

Shannon heard him move behind her, and then out of the corner of her eye she saw him put the copy of his precious bid proposal down on the table beside the buyer's contract. "What are you doing with that?"

"I'm leaving it with you."

Her eyes widened. "With me? You're leaving that copy of the proposal here? But, Garth, why?"

"Maybe because I'm trying to find some way of showing you that I trust you. Nor do I think you're stupid, even if you are a little naive. There's a big difference between stupid and naive, Shannon."

"Oh, Garth." Worriedly Shannon glanced at the contract and back at his calm face. "I don't think you should leave that here," she stated carefully.

"Why not?"

She waved a hand, trying to find the right words. "Because it scares me, if you want to know the truth. I don't ever want to see that proposal again. Every time I look at it I think about you finding it in my tote bag Sunday morning."

He caught her waving hand, holding it gently captive. "That's not what I want you to think when you look at it, Shannon. I want you to see it lying here in front of you for the next few days and think about the fact that I trust you with it. I can't undo the things I've said about you getting used by someone in my world, but I can at least prove I trust you. It's a start, honey. A foundation for us."

She went still, seeing the intensity in his gaze. "You don't trust very easily, do you, Garth?"

"No. But I'm willing to show I trust you."

Shannon gave a soft exclamation and went into his arms. "I'll take care of the proposal, Garth."

"I know you will." He stroked her back, his face in her hair. "By next Monday this whole mess will be finished. The sealed bids will have been turned over to Carstairs and then all we do is wait for the decision. Monday is the deadline." He paused, his hand still moving warmly on her spine. "I'll be back Friday evening."

Shannon forced a smile and looked up into his face. "I'll be here."

"I know. Honey, we've gotten off to a rocky start, but everything's going to work out. I know it will." He kissed her, his desire a volatile force held firmly in check by his self-control. Then he lifted his head. "I've got to get going."

"Yes." She didn't want him to leave. There were too many uncertainties left between them, too many things left unsaid. But Shannon also knew nothing was likely to get cleared up if he stayed. She walked him to the door and stood on the step as he slid into the Porsche and turned the key. Garth lifted his hand once in farewell and then he was gone.

Slowly Shannon went back into the cottage. She stood looking down at the bid proposal for several long moments, trying to comprehend exactly why Garth had left it. She certainly didn't want it in her house. It brought back too many miserable memories.

But Garth was trying to show her that he trusted her. Coming from him, it was a major step. It was more than just a simple, symbolic gesture. The proposal was important to him and it was clear someone had attempted to hand it over to a rival. Shannon, by virtue of being in the wrong place at the wrong time, could easily have been cast in the role of thief. Realistically speaking, Garth had had every right to be furious with her that morning he'd discovered it in her tote. Furthermore, Shannon admitted with a small groan, he'd had every right to assume she was guilty.

Apparently he was willing to prove he didn't think her guilty. She should value the gesture he was making, Shannon told herself. It was a major concession from a man who didn't completely trust anyone.

Shannon picked up the document and glanced around the kitchen. The copy of the proposal made her nervous. If she'd had her way, Garth would have taken it with him. She certainly didn't want it in her house. Restlessly she strolled from room to room, wondering where to store it.

In the end, she dropped the document into a silk-screened box used for storing her personal papers. The box was tacked to the inside of the closet door in her studio. When she shut the door, the box and the proposal were out of sight and out of mind. On Friday when Garth arrived she would hand the document back to him and tell him that, although she appreciated the gesture, she really didn't want to be responsible for the proposal any longer.

Taking a firm grip on herself, Shannon went back to work. Assuming the San Francisco buyer would accept the slightly revised contract, Shannon had a lot of work ahead of her. She put on her smock, attached the stencil design to the silk screen and inked the screen. Then she put the first square of canvas underneath the frame and picked up the squeegee. Fifteen minutes into the task, Shannon's mind finally began to clear. She concentrated on her work and refused to let herself think of the coming weekend.

The phone rang in the living room about one o'clock that afternoon. It was Annie O'Connor.

"I was just calling to see if you wanted to go to Verna's yuppie vegie play this evening. I know you didn't get the chance last weekend because you went to San Jose. Surely you're not going to pass up her masterpiece. Verna would be crushed."

Shannon laughed. "I wouldn't want to be responsible for injuring Verna's artistic ego. Are you and Dan both going?"

"Are you kidding? Every time I mention going to one of Verna's plays, Dan laughs his head off."

"I have to admit Garth wasn't too impressed with her version of *The Taming of the Shrew*. Verna is clearly ahead of her time, or at least ahead of most men. Okay, what time shall I pick you up?"

"Hmm. How about seven-thirty? That will give us time to park and find a good seat."

"See you then." Shannon hung up the phone thinking that it would be good to get out of the house that evening. She didn't want to sit by the phone and find herself waiting for Garth to call. Furthermore, if he did call, it might be good for Garth to find her out.

She was going to have to set the tone of this affair, Shannon told herself as she headed back to the studio. If she didn't, Garth would control it completely. If he had his way, he would tie her up in a nice neat package labeled Wife, and keep her firmly tucked away in a safe place where she couldn't get into any trouble. Then, on the weekends, he would take her out and play with her as if she were a toy.

Shannon frowned to herself. No, it wasn't fair to say he treated her as if she were a toy. You didn't go out of your way to prove to toys that you trusted them. Garth really was trying, she decided. But he had a long way to go. They were in the same situation they had been in before last weekend's fiasco. She was involved in a weekend affair with a man who still didn't want her sharing the major part of his life.

And knowing herself, Shannon thought grimly, she wouldn't take long to try once more to push her way into his other world. She would never be content to love a man who wouldn't share himself completely with her. It was just as it had been that first day on the beach. She was driven by a compulsion to know him and understand him. The present situation was only a temporary lull after a storm. Soon there would be another storm, and another after that. She would just keep pushing until Garth finally exploded and decided the relationship had no chance at all of working.

When that final day came, Shannon thought sadly, perhaps he would be grateful to her for not having taken him up on his proposal of marriage. At least he wouldn't be able to accuse her of having tricked him into a wedding on top of everything else.

VERNA MONTANA'S ALLEGORY of modern society as mirrored in a vegetable garden had a certain measure of originality going for it, but Annie and Shannon decided that, on the whole, it was just as well the men hadn't come with them to the play. The two women sat eating ice-cream sundaes at the parlor after the theatrical production had ended and tried to restrain their giggles.

"Dan would have had a fit. I'm sure he would have walked out during the first fifteen minutes. He has no patience with Verna's homemade plays. He thought *The Taming of the Shrew* was screwed up so badly he vowed he'd never sit through another production of hers," Annie confided.

"I have to admit Garth wasn't terribly impressed, either." Shannon concentrated on her ice cream, remembering how that evening had ended. "But on the whole I think Verna is better off sticking to the classics. She mangles them, but at least there's something to mangle. When she writes her own stuff, it's almost impossible to tell what's going on."

"Ah, well, who can define artistic vision?" Annie asked rhetorically. "Perhaps a hundred years from now her *Yuppie Vegies* will be considered a classic."

Shannon grinned. "I can just see some theatrical critic in the next century trying to analyze exactly what rutabagas had to do with twentieth-century culture. Verna may be on the cutting edge of artistic creation, but as far as I'm concerned, she can have the frontier all to herself. I'll be happy just to make a living with my silk screen."

Annie dug into the third scoop of ice cream in her bowl. "Speaking of which, when do you want me to sew up another batch of totes?"

"I can bring them over tomorrow, if that's all right. I'm sending the buyer twenty next Wednesday."

"You've signed the contract?" Annie asked with interest.

"Umm. After having it pointed out to me that I had almost signed away most of my rights."

"Uh-oh. Garth found something wrong with the contract?"

Shannon groaned. "It was very embarrassing, Annie. The truth was, I was so upset thinking about this past weekend that when I sat down to read the contract yesterday, I just wasn't concentrating. So naturally Garth blithely glances through it this morning and catches good old clause number six. I know I should have been more grateful, but somehow it just seemed to emphasize all the problems between us. He's going to insist on casting himself in the role of my protector, never letting me make any major decisions or get involved in the seamy side of life. Every time I turn around he's found some new way to look after me. He thinks my car is unsafe, and he's even making arrangements for me to have new locks installed. I'm to be especially protected from his big, tough, macho world in Silicon Valley. I'm definitely in over my head there." She smiled grimly. "I'm an adult and I want to be treated like one, Annie. But it seems like every other day something happens to make me look like a silly, foolish little female. Honestly, the way things are going, Garth has every reason to wonder how I've survived this long on my own."

"It's nice to have a man want to protect you," Annie mused thoughtfully.

"True, but how would you feel if Dan tried to exclude you from well over half his life because he said he wanted to 'protect' you from it?"

Annie chuckled. "I'd probably begin to suspect he was linked to the Mafia or something."

"Sometimes I get the impression that life in Silicon Valley bears a few striking resemblances to life in the Mafia," Shannon grumbled.

"Now you know how Mafia wives probably feel."

"Thanks, Annie, you're a great comfort to me."

SHANNON HAD LEFT the front-door light on earlier when she had left for the evening, and it glowed dully through the gathering fog as she parked her Fiat. The damp chill in the air made her clutch her shawl more closely around her shoulders as she climbed the steps and slipped her key into the lock.

Garth's plan to have new locks put on her doors and windows hadn't yet been put into effect. The locksmith he'd contacted had said he wouldn't be able to handle the job until the following week. Shannon wondered if she should fight harder against the whole project just on general principle. The truth was, she thought as she stepped into her front room, she really did need new locks. The ones on the cottage were very old, and there was no telling how many previous tenants had kept keys.

She grimaced as she switched on a light and dropped her tote onto the sofa. She was beginning to get paranoid herself. Until Garth had pointed out the age of the locks she hadn't worried about them in the least.

Idly she wandered into the kitchen and thought about making herself a cup of tea. It was almost ten o'clock, but she didn't feel sleepy. She could get in a couple of hours of silk-screening before she went to bed. Shannon switched on the kettle and waited for the water to boil. Then she poured it over the tea bag and headed for the studio while she waited for the brew to steep.

She paused as she stopped in front of the studio door. She hadn't remembered closing it earlier. Then again, perhaps she had. Who remembered for certain whether a door had been closed? Shrugging, Shannon opened it and stepped inside the darkened room.

She felt something was wrong even as she groped automatically for the light switch. The soft, heavy movement to her right brought a scream to her lips as she frantically tried to back out of the room.

Her hand never reached the switch and Shannon never made good her escape from the room. There was a muffled curse and a man's arm was suddenly tightening around her throat, choking off her scream.

"Not a word," the voice grated, sounding thick and raspy behind a layer of fabric. The man was hooded. "Not one damn word, you little bitch. You hear me?"

Shannon didn't bother to respond. She was struggling desperately, her nails digging for purchase on the arm around her throat.

"Stop it," the intruder snarled as Shannon managed to land a blow with the heel of her foot. "Just stop struggling and pay attention. I'm here for the bid."

"Ummmph?" Shannon shoved at him, trying to claw his neck.

"The Carstairs bid, damn it. That's all I want. Just hand over the bid and I'll get out of here!" He swore again as she scraped her nails across the back of his hands. "I just want the bid. I know you've got your own game going, but I've got to complete my deal. My client will nail me to the wall if I don't. Hell, I'm willing to pay you for the thing. It won't be anything close to what you'd get by selling it yourself, but at least it will be something. Be reasonable."

"Reasonable!" Shannon managed to choke out the words. "Are you out of your head?"

"Look, you had some bad luck. Your deal isn't going to go through. It's tough, I know. But I haven't got any extra sympathy to spare, understand? I've got my own problems. Now hand over the bid you lifted the night of the party. It had to be you. I knew as soon as he told me the stupid tote bag was empty that I'd put it in the wrong one. *Where is it?*"

"I don't know what you're talking about," Shannon gasped.

"The hell you don't. I want that bid package, lady, and you're going to hand it over to me."

She couldn't feel any steel against her throat and as far as Shannon could tell, her attacker wasn't holding a gun. He probably assumed that since she was only a woman, he didn't need a weapon. Or perhaps Silicon Valley spies didn't routinely carry weapons. Desperately she tried to think.

"All right," she hissed. "I'll give you what you want. Stop choking me to death."

The arm around her throat loosened somewhat and she sucked in air. "The light . . ."

"Forget the light. We don't need it. Now where's the bid package?"

"Closet," she got out painfully. "Other side of the room."

"Move." He dragged her across the room, feeling in the dark for the closet door handle. The door came open with a squeak. Even in the shadows it was possible to see how crowded the interior of the closet was. "Now where the hell is it?"

"I'll get it. Just let me go, will you? Believe me, I'm not going to risk my life over a stupid bid proposal."

Her assailant's hand reluctantly loosened a bit more. "No tricks."

"I don't know any. I'm just a naive little artsy-craftsy type. Haven't you figured that out yet?" Shannon's hand swept out across her worktable as she stepped away from the man who had been holding her. Her fingers touched the small knife she used for cutting her stencils and closed around it.

"Naive, my ass. You're one shrewd little cookie, baby. Ordinarily, I'd tell you just how good I think you are, but I haven't got time tonight. Get the bid!"

Shannon didn't bother to answer. Her hand whipped around, slamming the short point of the knife into the intruder's shoulder. She put every ounce of strength into it, gritting her teeth with a savagery that would have astonished her if she'd been aware of it.

The man screamed, probably as much out of surprise as pain. The blade was only about half an inch long and couldn't have gone very deep. But he was truly rattled by the unexpected assault and instinctively he leaped out of the way, slapping a hand across his wound. In the darkness he had no way of knowing if she were getting set for another stabbing blow.

But Shannon wasn't trying for another blow. She was already lunging for the box of papers tacked inside the closet door, wrenching it free before the man had realized what was happening.

"Damn you, come back here!" The rage in the intruder's voice was palpable as Shannon swept past him, clutching the box. She raced through the living room and an instant later was out the front door into the sheltering safety of the fog.

9

THERE WAS NO TIME to grab the car keys, no time to start the Fiat even if she'd had the keys ready in her hand. Shannon dashed around the corner of the cottage, aware that the intruder was already lunging through the front door after her.

The fog broke and swirled around her, offering concealment as well as danger. She knew her way around the surrounding terrain, but in the darkness there were countless small hazards waiting to trip the unwary.

"Wait, damn you! We can make a deal."

The shout was too close behind her. Shannon couldn't see her pursuer, but she knew he was very near. She went still as she heard the blundering approach of the man. He passed within a couple of yards, and Shannon held her breath, clutching the box of papers. A moment later he had veered off in another direction. She sensed his desperation and wondered for the first time just how important the bid proposal was. What kind of a world did Garth operate in where people attacked others for a business document?

The questions as well as the answers would have to wait. Like it or not, the proposal had been left in her keeping and Shannon had every intention of guarding it. She edged toward the bluff that overlooked the sea, trying to remember where the rocks and trees were. The last thing she needed at the moment was a collision with one of the scruffy, wind-twisted trees that dotted the area.

Shannon could hear the roiling surf as she worked her way toward the cliff edge. The crashing water was reassuring. The sound of it would cover any noise she was making. On the negative side, it also disguised the sounds of pursuit. It was impossible to tell how close the man was. It would be just her luck, Shannon thought, to run into him somewhere in this soup.

Her best bet was to get down on the beach. Chances were the intruder would have no way of guessing which way she had gone once she made her way down the short cliff.

"I'm willing to talk, lady." The raspy voice was hard to hear over the sounds of the sea. It came from the left but not from nearby. "We can split the profits. But that bid has to go to my client. *I must have it.*"

The urgency in the man's voice was unnerving. Shannon quickened her step, nearly stumbling over a clump of tough vegetation that had dug its roots deep into the rocky soil. She held her breath again as she regained her balance, wondering frantically if her pursuer had heard her stifled gasp.

When there was no detectable pounding of footsteps, Shannon scrambled over the edge of the shallow cliff, slipping and sliding on the pebbly surface.

Then, with an undignified thump, she found herself in a tangled heap at the bottom. The last few feet had not been negotiated with her usual finesse. But she still had the box in her hand as she staggered and turned immediately to the right.

The tide was coming in and as she made her way over the uneven beach, Shannon hugged the cliff wall. Occasionally her shoes got splashed by a foaming wave she couldn't even see, and she realized how easy it would be to get disoriented. But the cliff gave her a point of reference. With gathering certainty she moved toward the far end of the beach and tried not to wonder which way the intruder was taking.

Fifteen minutes and three unpleasant falls later, Shannon sensed the looming cliff at the end of the beach. The path to the top was somewhere close. Heaven knew she had used it a number of times. Through a momentary clearing in the fog she spotted the familiar tumble of rocks that marked the bottom of the path. With a sigh of relief, Shannon started making her way upward. When she emerged, she knew just where she would be and that was considerably more than her pursuer could possibly guess.

The cliff was steeper here than it was down at her end of the beach, and Shannon had to use one hand to grab for support in several slippery places. She kept the box tucked under her other arm and grimly fought her way to the top. By the time she reached her goal, she was panting from exertion and the adrenaline-enhanced fear that was still roaring through her veins.

She decided she really wasn't cut out to play the game of corporate espionage.

Taking a deep breath, Shannon started walking inland from the edge of the cliff. Her destination lay a short distance away. By traveling along the curving beach, she had shortened the distance she would have had to negotiate had she taken the road. Through the fog she could see the welcome porch light of the house Annie O'Connor shared with Dan Turcott.

A few minutes later Shannon was pounding on the front door. Leaning against the wall, still grasping the box tightly in front of her, Shannon breathed a sigh of relief as she heard sounds of movement from within. A moment later the door was opened, and Dan Turcott stood frowning under the porch light. He had obviously been in bed and had taken time to pull on only a pair of jeans.

"What the hell? Shannon! For crying out loud. What are you doing here?"

"It's a short, pithy story. If you'll let me in I'll tell it to you."

"Come on inside." He reached out to catch hold of her arm and tug her over the threshold. Shannon needed no real urging. "Annie!" Dan turned his head to shout down the short hall to the bedroom. "It's Shannon. She looks like something the cat dragged in. Better get up and give me a hand."

"Don't worry, I'm not going to collapse," Shannon declared stoutly and then promptly fell into a chair. "On the other hand, maybe I am. Good grief, what a night. First yuppie vegies and now this. I used to lead such a quiet life."

"Shannon! What on earth happened?" Annie was knotting a robe around her pregnant stomach as she came down the hall. Concern etched her soft face as she turned on the living room lights. "Are you all right?"

"I think she needs a shot of something with a kick. I'll see if we've got any brandy left." Dan stepped into the kitchen. "What's this all about, Shannon? Do I need to call the cops?"

Shannon nodded as she leaned gratefully back into the chair cushions. "I'm afraid so. There was someone in my cottage when I got home tonight."

"Oh, my God." Annie picked up the phone. "You're not hurt?"

"Just a little skinned up from a midnight hike on the beach. I managed to get out the front door and down to the water."

Dan emerged from the kitchen and reached out to take the phone from Annie. "Here, I'll do that. See that she drinks this."

Shannon accepted the water glass that had been half-filled with brandy and quickly outlined the story for Annie as Dan made his call to the local authorities. He broke into her tale at one point with a quick question.

"Gibson says he'll be right out to have a look. Wants to know if the guy is armed."

"I don't think so, but I couldn't swear to it. I didn't see any sign of a gun or a knife. But tell Gibson that I did take a chunk out of the man's arm. His right arm, I think."

"A chunk?"

"I stabbed him with the blade I use to cut stencils. It won't have done much damage, but the wound might be useful for identification."

Dan raised his eyebrows in silent comment and then repeated the information to the man on the other end of the line. A moment later he hung up the phone. "Now I suppose I'd better call Garth."

Shannon looked at him. "I suppose so, but there's not much point in rushing the call, is there? What can he do from San Jose? He's four hours away."

"He'll want to know what's happened," Dan pointed out gently. "I get the feeling he spends a lot of time worrying about you. What's that you're holding on your lap?"

Shannon blinked and glanced down at the silk-screen-printed container she had been clutching. "Something that belongs to Garth," she said slowly. "The intruder wanted it tonight. It's the reason he broke into my cottage."

Annie came up off the sofa where she had been sitting while getting Shannon to drink the brandy. Her expression was that of an avenging angel. Imperiously she took the receiver out of Dan's hand.

"I," Annie announced, "will make the call to Garth Sheridan."

THE RINGING OF THE PHONE beside the bed did not rouse Garth from a deep sleep. He'd spent the evening doing a great deal of thinking, and when he'd finally undressed and dropped into bed, his mind hadn't switched off. He'd been lying awake with his arms folded behind his head on the pillow for almost an hour when the jarring sound of the phone disturbed his restless, brooding mood.

His first thought was that the caller might be Shannon, and Garth grabbed the receiver with a sense of urgency. He wasn't prepared for the scolding voice on the other end of the line. Annie O'Connor identified herself immediately, and in no uncertain terms launched into her description of what had happened to Shannon.

"Are you listening, Garth Sheridan? Shannon could have been raped or killed tonight. What's all this fine talk about protecting her? All that jazz about it being a man's duty to take care of his woman? Who was it who gave Dan and me a lecture on the necessity of getting married because a man had an obligation to protect his woman and child? I've got news for you, Garth—telling Shannon to put new locks on her door and to give up driving a small sports car does not constitute protecting her. A man who cared about her would be with her seven days a week, not just on the weekends. At least my Dan doesn't leave me alone five days a week and expect me to cope with intruders, broken plumbing, car problems and heaven knows what else while he's gone."

Cold fear washed through Garth as he listened to the tirade. "Annie, stop for a moment. Please. Is Shannon all right?"

"All right? Yes, she's all right, if you can count being attacked by an intruder and having to flee into the night as being all right. She's sitting here on my sofa right this minute, and do you know what she's holding on her lap, Garth? That stupid bid proposal you left with her."

"The bid package?" Garth was stunned.

"It's what the intruder wanted," Annie told him. "It's what he nearly strangled her trying to get. But she didn't give it to him. She stabbed the guy in the arm and raced out of the cottage with your damn proposal. The next thing Dan and I know she's standing on our front doorstep after having run for Lord knows how far in the fog."

"The cops . . ."

"Dan has already phoned the cops," Annie informed him with blunt satisfaction. "Someone had to do it, and you certainly weren't around to take the responsibility, were you?"

"Annie," he interrupted desperately, "let me talk to Shannon."

"She's drinking brandy, trying to recover. What good will talking to you do? You're two hundred miles away. Besides, I think I hear the local law arriving. We're going to be very busy explaining things to them for a while. Why don't you call back later, Garth?"

She hung up the phone before Garth could tell her he wasn't about to call back later and that he intended to speak to Shannon immediately. Angrily he started to redial and then realized he didn't know Annie and Dan's number. Getting it from information took precious minutes. By the time the phone was ringing in Annie's cottage, Garth was rigid with tension. He was ready for Annie's righteous vehemence when someone finally picked up the receiver on the other end.

"Just a damn minute, Annie. Don't you dare hang up on me. I want to speak to Shannon now."

"Hi, Garth," Shannon said wearily.

"Shannon? I thought it would be Annie again. What the hell's going on?"

"I'm rather busy at the moment, Garth. The cops have a lot of questions for me to answer. I'll have to call you later, okay?"

"No, wait, it's not okay...." Frantically he tried to keep her on the line, but he knew she was about to hang up again. "Damn it, Shannon, hold on, I've got a few questions of my own."

"You don't have to worry about the bid package, Garth. I've got it."

"Shannon!"

The phone clicked in his ear, and Garth slammed his own receiver back into its cradle. Helplessly he stared out into the darkened garden beyond the bedroom window. His insides were twisting with rage and frustration. Two hundred miles away. He was sitting here two hundred miles away while Shannon went through hell. Garth got to his feet, wanting to knock a hole through the bedroom wall, anything to relieve the helpless tension. Grimly he brought his simmering fury back under control.

It was nearly one o'clock in the morning. If he left immediately he could be at the coast shortly before five. Hell, driving at this time of night he should be able to do a lot better than that. Garth reached for a pair of jeans and a shirt. He was going to go out of his mind sitting here. He had to get to Shannon.

The drive to the coast seemed to last forever, although Garth had never made better time. He had the highway to himself, and the Porsche sliced through the night as if it owned it. Garth drove with ruthless efficiency and little regard for the speed limit. His only goal was to get to Shannon. Three hours later he was pulling into her driveway. He hadn't encountered any fog until the last few miles, but now the mist was annoyingly thick. The light over her front door was on, and the Fiat was parked nearby. There was no sign of activity within the cottage. She'd be in bed, Garth decided as he got out of the Porsche. By now the police would have come and gone.

When there was no answer to his knock, Garth's inner tension peaked again. Belatedly he realized Shannon might have stayed the rest of the night with Annie and Dan.

"Shannon?" He pounded once more and then loped back to the Porsche. He remembered the cottage

Shannon had pointed out as the one belonging to Annie and Dan. Shoving the keys back into the ignition,
Garth put the car in gear and slammed the vehicle
onto the narrow road.

SHANNON HEARD the pounding knock on Annie and
Dan's front door quite clearly because she was sleeping on the sofa in the living room. Dazedly she awoke,
remembering vaguely that she wasn't in her own
home. The crashing knock on the door came again,
and this time Garth's voice accompanied it.

"Dan? It's Sheridan. Open up. Is Shannon with
you?"

Shannon shook off her sleepy haze and sat up on
the sofa. "I'm coming, Garth." She traipsed to the
door, yawning widely as she opened it. For a moment
she simply stared at his haggard expression as he stood
beneath the porch light. "Hi."

"Hi, yourself," he muttered, reaching out to catch
hold of her shoulders with both hands. His gaze raked
her from head to foot. "Are you all right?"

"I'm okay."

"Hell, Shannon, I thought I would go crazy after
Annie called." He pulled her into his arms, locking her
securely to him. "I was so damn far away."

Shannon's voice was muffled against his shirt as she
found her face pushed firmly into his chest. "I know."

Dan's voice came from the hall doorway. "Well, you
made pretty good time, Garth. I didn't expect to see

you for another hour or so." He yawned. "Need a place to sleep?"

Garth shook his head. "I'll take Shannon back to the cottage." He looked at the other man over the top of Shannon's head, keeping her close. "Thanks, Dan. I owe you."

There was a curious smile in Dan's voice as he answered. "You don't owe me a thing. Shannon's the one who saved your bid package for you."

"Damn the bid package," Garth said with great feeling. "It was worrying about Shannon that drove me out of my mind."

"I know just how you must have felt," Dan offered calmly. "Maybe you'd better take your own advice and marry the woman."

Garth's voice hardened. "I told you I've already offered." His hands tightened on Shannon as she tried to lift her head.

"What good would being married have done?" she managed, the words still muffled because of the way he was holding her. "You'd still have been in San Jose tonight."

It was Annie who responded to that comment. She'd materialized in the hall behind Dan. "Precisely my point," she murmured. "Good night, Garth. Take her home and get some sleep. You look like you need it."

Garth didn't need a second urging. He glanced down at Shannon. Seeing her still wearing her jeans and a pullover, he said, "Let's get going. We've got a lot of talking to do." ·

She yawned delicately and then slipped out of his arms to find her shoes. When she came back toward him she was holding the box of papers that contained the Carstairs bid. "Here. I almost forgot. You can have it. I really would rather not be responsible for it any longer."

Without looking at the document she was pulling from the box and handing to him, Garth took it. The expression in his eyes was raw. "Shannon, I never meant for anything like this to happen. It never occurred to me that you would be in danger because of this."

"I know." She turned to wave good-night to Annie and Dan. "Thanks, you two. I'll see you tomorrow. I mean today. It is today, isn't it? How time flies when you're having fun. I'm ready, Garth."

He walked her out to the car and put her into the passenger seat with grave care. Shannon smiled fleetingly.

"I'm not an invalid. I'm really very much all right."

"You may not be an invalid but I feel like a basket case." He slid behind the wheel and started the engine with a disgusted shake of his head. "I never want to go through anything like this again."

"I'll second that. You must be exhausted after that drive."

"I couldn't go to sleep now if my life depended on it," he told her as he drove back to the cottage. "I'd like some explanations and answers, honey. I know you're tired and you've been through a lot, but . . ."

"I don't mind. It'll be dawn soon, anyway, and I always was an early riser."

"Just tell me what happened right from the start."

She did. When they reached the cottage Garth made tea, and twenty minutes later she concluded her tale. "The police said they searched the area, but with all the fog it was impossible to find anything useful. Not even a car. Personally, I think whoever it was was long gone by the time the cops got here. The same fog that made it hard for the authorities to find anything also made it tough for that turkey to find me. Thank God."

Garth massaged the back of his neck as he sat nursing his tea. "You're sure he wanted that copy of the bid proposal?"

Shannon nodded. "No doubt about it."

"I don't get it. How could he even know you had it?"

"Beats me." She sipped her tea, realizing that it was very comforting to have Garth here at last. She shouldn't get accustomed to the feeling, Shannon reminded herself. "No, wait a minute. He said something about having realized he'd put it in the wrong tote at the party."

"I haven't told a single soul about that second copy of the bid. The only one who knows about it is the guy who copied and stole it in the first place."

"He kept mentioning a 'client.'"

"Yeah, of course there's a client. Must be someone who's willing to pay well."

"Or someone who's dangerous," Shannon mused. "I got the feeling the guy in my studio was nervous, maybe even downright scared about not being able to deliver. Said he'd make a deal with me. Split the profits."

Garth considered that. "I'll have to call Balley immediately."

"Who's Balley?"

"An industrial security firm. They specialize in this kind of thing, and I've used them before. They're the firm that supplies my guards at Sherilectronics. They're good. I put them on this right away on Monday. But when I told them to look into the situation I was concerned only with finding out who might have made the copy of the bid. I didn't think the package itself was a danger."

"Why not?" Shannon asked curiously.

"Because I didn't think things would go this far, damn it!" Garth's mood caused him to explode in an unexpected burst of rage. "I'd intercepted the stolen bid. I figured that would be the end of it. A smart thief would cut his losses at that point and figure the situation was too hot. Besides, time has just about run out for him. The facts and figures in the bid package are only useful to a rival up to the time when the bids have to be turned in to Carstairs. This is early Thursday morning. All the competitive proposals go to Carstairs on Monday. After that, it doesn't matter who sees the bid package."

Shannon frowned. "Weren't you concerned that there might be another copy of the bid package floating around? The only hard part was copying it the first time because you had so much security in force. Once the thief had made one copy of the original, he could have taken it to any photocopy shop and had another made. Heck, he could have had ten others made."

"If that were the case, there wasn't a damn thing I could have done about it. But it's not likely that whoever stole the first copy would make any more if he could avoid it. It would be dangerous and highly incriminating if the document turned up in his possession. At any rate, I think we can safely assume now that there's only one copy. Otherwise, the thief wouldn't have been so desperate to get back the one in your possession. My guess is that the transaction was supposed to take place the night of the party and when the copy of the bid disappeared, there wasn't another to take its place. Which," Garth finished roughly, "is why the jerk came looking for it. But I still can't figure out how he knew you had it."

"I told you. He seemed to know who owned the tote bag," Shannon said dryly. "When it disappeared and the bid with it, he assumed I'd decided to work my own scam."

Garth stared at her from suddenly narrowed eyes. "Your own scam?"

"A perfectly logical assumption for him to make, don't you think?" she asked with a flippancy she was far from feeling.

Garth looked as if someone had hit him in the stomach. "Oh, my God, Shannon."

"I know. I was a little shaken myself."

Garth sat quietly for a moment, dealing with the ramifications of what she had just said. Shannon watched him, knowing he was working through some things in his mind and when he was finished she was going to find herself facing a formidable creature. Mentally she braced herself.

"I've got to get back to San Jose," Garth finally stated.

"I realize that. You've got a business to run. With that proposal due in to Carstairs by Monday, you can't be running around the countryside."

Garth nodded thoughtfully. "This whole thing is too hot. There are too many unknown factors here, including the possibility that whoever is responsible for the theft is getting very desperate. It looks like it's a much bigger mess than I originally figured. I need to be where I can keep an eye on Sherilectronics. I've got to find out what's going on and who's trying to betray me. There's nothing I can do here on the coast."

"Of course," Shannon said quietly.

"And I need you where I can keep an eye on you," he concluded. "You'd better pack a bag, Shannon. I'm taking you back to San Jose with me."

Shannon's cup came down on the saucer with a small crash. Her eyes widened in protest and astonishment. "Garth, I can't go back with you. I've got the first shipment of tote bags to finish. Even with Annie's help it's going to take me right through the weekend to finish the sewing process. Then I have to pack and ship them."

"Shannon, your neck is a lot more important than your tote bags!"

"My tote bags are as important to me as Sherilectronics is to you, Garth. I'm not going to blow my first big order by failing to meet the deadline. I have to stay here and finish them."

Garth surged to his feet, pacing across the kitchen with a scowl on his face. "I can't leave you here alone," he bit out.

"I can't come with you."

"Damn it," he grated, swinging around to glower at her, "for the past few weeks you've done nothing but try to push your way into my San Jose life. Now that I'm offering to take you back with me, you dig in your heels."

"I don't call dragging me back to San Jose so that you can keep your eagle eye on me an example of sharing your world with me, Garth. You're just trying to kill two birds with one stone. You want to keep tabs on Sherilectronics during this crucial juncture and you feel you should also keep tabs on me."

He planted both hands on the table in front of her and leaned forward. "You bet your sweet tail I feel obliged to keep an eye on you. After what happened here last night, what do you expect?"

"You're not responsible for me, Garth."

"The hell I'm not."

"We're involved in a weekend affair. That's the sum total of the arrangement, and frankly that doesn't say a great deal. It certainly doesn't imply that you should be excessively concerned about my well-being. I'll exercise due caution until Monday. Take your stupid bid package back to San Jose and worry about finding the thief. I'll be fine."

"Now you listen to me, Shannon Raine." Each word was harsh with leashed fury. "I've had a rough night and a long drive. I'm in no mood to put up with your artistic temperament. You're going to be reasonable and rational about this. And that means you will pack a bag and come back to San Jose with me."

Shannon was almost overwhelmed by the force of the command in him. It took all her nerve to hold her ground. "I don't know how to tell you this, Garth, but for some reason I've lost all interest in San Jose and what it represents. You're welcome to it. And you don't have to worry, I won't be pushing you anymore to make me a part of your life there. I've decided I don't particularly like your Silicon Valley world, Garth. I agree with you. We should keep our relationship limited to the weekends."

"You're upset and you're not thinking logically, honey. Stop arguing with me and trust me to do what's best for you."

"You don't know me well enough to know what's best for me. And if the only time we see each other is on an occasional weekend, you probably won't ever get to the point where you know what's good for me." She was getting hysterical and she knew it. Shannon reined in her volatile emotions, striving to bring them under control. She had to keep calm or Garth would take over.

"You must see that I've got to get back to San Jose," Garth said through gritted teeth. "Someone is trying to betray me. I've got to stop him, and I don't have a chance of doing that if I stay here."

"Go."

"I'm not leaving you here alone!"

"I'm not coming with you."

Garth's eyes were twin pools of ice as he glared down at her. Then quite suddenly he was straightening and heading out of the kitchen. Shannon watched warily as he disappeared into the living room. "Garth?"

She got up and followed as far as the kitchen door. Garth was dialing her phone. "Garth, what are you doing? Who are you calling?"

"Balley Security. I'm going to have them assign someone to watch this cottage night and day until I can get back here. If you insist on staying here alone,

Shannon, I'm going to make sure you have a bodyguard."

Shannon was floored. "Garth, you can't do that. I
won't stand for it!"

"You," he told her coolly, "don't have any choice."

10

THE BALLEY OPERATIVE was as discreet as possible.
Shannon gave him credit for that much, at least. But
every time she glanced out her window she could see
his incredibly nondescript car sitting across the road.
The figure inside the vehicle was that of a man.
Slightly balding, slightly built and slightly self-
effacing, he had been quite polite in the face of Shannon's obvious disgust with the entire situation. He had
introduced himself to Garth and Shannon as Ted
Walters, and physically he was as nondescript as his
car. Shannon had gloomily decided that was probably an asset in his business.

"Well, at least he's not going to be baby-sitting me
inside the house," Shannon remarked irritably as
Garth prepared to take his leave. It had taken Ted
Walters nearly two hours to arrive from one of Balley's branch offices. Garth had stayed with Shannon
until the security man was in place.

"I don't want him inside your cottage," Garth told
her. "I want him out there where he can keep an eye
on things. That way he won't be underfoot. You'll be
able to go about your normal routine without being
aware of him."

"Oh, sure. And when my friends ask me why a beige Ford has been parked across the street for a couple of days I can always tell them he's a traveling salesman."

Garth reacted to the gibe. It was the first time he had responded with anything but quiet, inflexible patience to Shannon's increasingly angry comments. Perhaps it had been his cold determination that had fed her sense of outrage. If he had argued with her, even yelled at her, she might have at least gotten some satisfaction from yelling back. Instead he had simply made the arrangements he wanted and refused to discuss them with her. Now he was almost ready to leave, and Shannon had reached the end of her own patience. She stood facing Garth with her hands on her hips, her head thrown back and the light of battle in her eyes. Garth watched her with considering eyes for a moment and then stepped forward. He gripped her shoulders, keeping his voice dangerously soft.

"You will not tell your friends anything, Shannon. There is nothing they need to know. This will all be over in a couple of days. With luck, by the weekend. I'm going to go back to San Jose and clean up this mess. In the meantime, I don't want to take any chances on this end. Logically, you should be in the clear by now. Whoever's behind this must know the police were called and that I'm alerted. But just in case, Walters and his relief man are going to keep an eye on this place. You don't have to worry about anything except getting that damn tote bag order filled. It seems to be the most important thing in your life, so stop sniping at me and get busy." He dropped his hands from her shoulders and turned toward the door.

"Garth, wait . . ." Shannon sucked in her breath on a sob of frustation and hurried after him. She caught up with him at the door. He stopped and faced her, eyes unreadable. "Be careful," she whispered. "Please, be careful."

For the first time since she had refused to return to San Jose with him, Garth's expression softened. He touched her cheek. "I'll be careful. Stop worrying, Shannon." He leaned over and brushed his mouth across hers. "I'll be back on Friday evening."

He was gone before she could think of anything else to say. Standing at the window, Shannon watched the Porsche slip out onto the road and disappear. For a few moments she remained where she was, trying to understand the emotional storm that seemed to have her in its grip.

She loved him, Shannon thought, but how could she tolerate the constant suspicion and betrayal that seemed so much a part of his world? It was true Garth had tried to keep her free of that side of his life, but Shannon had gotten involved anyway. He couldn't shield her forever—and she didn't want him to. She had to be able to share his world if she was going to continue the relationship. She had learned enough during the past few weeks to know she couldn't be just a weekend lover or a weekend wife.

Slowly Shannon turned away from the window and headed toward her studio. Working with a skill that was automatic, she set up the screen, applied the ink and went to work on the last portion of the canvas squares. Then she removed the wet canvas and put another in its place. Time passed as she labored, and when Shannon happened to glance at her watch she was vaguely surprised to find it was nearly noon. She wondered if Ted Walters was getting bored or hungry.

Stretching to get the kinks out of her back muscles, Shannon straightened away from the silk-screen frame and decided to make herself a bite to eat. Maybe she would show how broad-minded she could be and offer Walters a sandwich or a cup of coffee.

She wandered into the kitchen and opened the refrigerator door. The only things that looked appealing were a slab of cheese and some sprouts. Locating a loaf of whole-grain bread, Shannon set about making two thick sandwiches. Then she made coffee and poured a healthy dose of it into a large mug. Security guards probably didn't drink tea.

Feeling enormously kind and forgiving, Shannon picked up one sandwich and the oversize mug and opened the front door. After all, it was unfair to blame poor Ted Walters for what amounted to merely doing his job. It was hardly his fault Garth had demanded the services of a full-time baby-sitter for her. She smiled benignly as she opened the door, hoping to make amends for her less than polite greeting earlier.

Prepared for a hungry, grateful man sitting out a solitary vigil, Shannon was startled to see that the nondescript car was no longer parked across the road. For a moment she stood in the doorway, glancing around to see if Ted Walters had changed his location. There was no sign of him or the car.

Shannon closed the door again and went back to the kitchen to eat her own lunch. Perhaps security types had regular coffee and meal breaks, just like normal employees. The man hadn't knocked on her door with a request to use her plumbing facilities all morning. He might have taken a fifteen-minute break to search out his own now.

Deciding it really didn't matter to her, Shannon finished her meal and considered a short walk on the beach. She felt the need for some exercise before going back to work. Silk-screening was hard, physical labor that often left her muscles cramped and tired.

The day had turned out beautifully. All traces of fog had evaporated. In another couple of hours it would be genuinely warm. Shannon made her way down the short cliff to the rough beach and thought about her mad dash across the same territory the previous evening. She realized she had been lucky not to take a couple of really bad falls on the uneven ground.

Setting off toward the far end of the beach, Shannon walked briskly. The exercise felt good, clearing away some of the cobwebs from her troubled mind and loosening her muscles. Deliberately she considered her future.

She knew she was going to have to make some harsh decisions. True, she was in love, but no amount of passion was going to sustain her in the kind of relationship Garth seemed to want. Furthermore, the uncertainty she always felt when she tried to assess his emotions was as strong as ever. Valiantly, she tried to mentally list the pros and cons of her situation.

There could be no doubt that he desired her, Shannon thought wistfully. And she sensed that his possessiveness and feelings of responsibility toward her went deep. The fact that he had managed to convince himself she hadn't stolen the bid package was heartening. Shannon smiled grimly. All things considered, it was actually pretty remarkable that Garth had given her the benefit of the doubt. Judging from what she knew of his world and his past, she was aware that it would have been logical for him to assume the worst.

Of course, having him think of her as simply too unsophisticated and naive to know how to go about seducing and betraying him wasn't exactly a compliment. Shannon rebelled at the idea of being declared somewhat innocent by reason of stupidity. And as much as she loved him, she rebelled, too, at the notion of marriage to a man who wanted to keep her stashed away until the weekends. He wasn't just trying to protect her, Shannon knew intuitively. Garth was really trying to protect himself. He had practically admitted as much. He wanted to be able to use Shannon as a retreat and a refuge, not realizing that by so doing he was relegating her to only a minimal role in his life.

Not that she couldn't comprehend and even sympathize with his desire for an alternative to his working world, Shannon thought with an inner sigh. But she wondered whether he could learn to ever really love her as long as she was kept on the fringes of his life. A part of her clung to the knowledge that he wanted her to love him. She tried to tell herself it was a hopeful sign. But another more practical voice warned Shannon that she needed to be loved completely in return. She wasn't sure how long it would take a man like Garth to trust her and himself deeply enough to allow himself to risk loving her.

In many ways she had been right about him that first morning when she had followed him down to the beach and invited him to her dinner party. Garth's dark, brooding spirit was as complex and remote as that of any poet or writer. Unfortunately for her, she still felt the same compulsion to force her way past the barriers he was so good at erecting. It would be simpler, Shannon thought, if she could write Garth Sheridan off as a negative experience. But writing off the man you loved was easier said than done.

The depressing train of thought came to an abrupt
halt as Shannon shook herself free of it. She would not
give up on this man. Not yet. Maybe not ever. She
loved him too much to allow failure.

Somehow, some way, she would find a path that led
to the inner sanctum of Garth's emotions. The man
had potential, she told herself resolutely. And she was
the persevering type. She would continue to pursue
him until he fell in love with her. And once he had ac-
knowledged that much, she was certain she could start
to change his life. Because it would take no less than
a major life-style change for Garth to become the kind
of lover and husband Shannon wanted.

With a new feeling of calm determination, Shannon wheeled around and started back up the beach.
She had gone only a few paces when she realized she
was not alone. For a moment she could not identify
the man who had just descended the cliff at the point
where she had earlier. He was too far away for her to
see his face. But something about the way he moved
toward her was alarming. It was also familiar.

Shannon halted, seriously considering a scramble
up the steeper portion of the cliff wall that was to her
right. Frowning, she edged toward it. She had no real
cause for panic, she told herself. It must have been the
lingering effects of her experience last night. Her hand
was braced on a jutting shoulder, and she was search-
ing for a foothold when the approaching man called

to her. She recognized the voice at the same moment she got a good look at his features.

"Wes! What on earth are you doing here?" Astonished at McIntyre's presence, Shannon came away from the cliff and waited. A sudden thought struck her. "Garth didn't send you to keep an eye on me, too, did he?" she asked wryly. "One bodyguard is enough."

"No, Shannon, I'm not here to protect you." Wes came to a halt a few feet away, his handsome face set in taut lines that changed his whole appearance. He suddenly didn't seem to look at all like the easygoing man Shannon had met in Garth's office. "I'm here to make a deal with you. You're clever. I'll admit that. In the beginning, I made the mistake of totally underestimating you. I know better now, and I'm willing to put this on a businesslike basis. We have to cooperate, you and I. There's no choice."

"A deal!" And then it hit her. Shannon's eyes narrowed as she absorbed the implications of what he had said. Too late she realized she ought to have made the dash up the cliff. "You're the one," she got out, her voice tight with anger. She was distantly grateful for the raw edge of fury that was lacing her words. It was far more bracing than the whimper of panic. "You tried to change your voice last night but I recognize it now. You're betraying Garth. You were the one who searched my place last night."

"I'm going to be damn lucky not to get an infection from that knife you used." Wes gingerly touched his arm with the opposite hand. He frowned bitterly. "I'd never have guessed you were the violent type and I'm usually damn good at analyzing people. No wonder you fooled Garth. You're a very talented actress, Shannon. The sweet, unworldly artist routine was the one kind of act he wouldn't have been expecting. I'd like to know how you set it up, though. Just out of curiosity, you understand. How did you know where and when he'd be taking that trip over here to the coast? Your sources must be good, Shannon. Very well placed."

"Don't be stupid, Wes. I'm not working with anyone. Your own mind must be very twisted to make you think everyone else is just as warped as you are."

He grimaced. "Don't tell me you're going to carry the act out to the end? It can't last, you know. Sooner or later, Sheridan will figure out who was behind the theft and when that time comes, the only safe place to be is out of his reach. Believe me, I know."

"Is that where you intended to be?" Shannon asked scornfully. "Out of reach after you'd completed the sale of that bid package?"

"Very much out of reach," he returned coolly. "Who's your client?"

"I haven't got a client, you idiot."

He shrugged. "All right, you don't have to tell me. I just thought the information might be interesting."

"Who's yours?"

"Kenyon."

Shannon sighed. "That figures. You were supposed to make the transfer at the party that night, I assume?"

"It seemed the best time. You don't know Sheridan. When he slaps a security blanket on Sherilectronics, the way he did while this bid package was being worked out, he's very, very thorough. It would have been risky for me to meet Kenyon at any time during the past couple of weeks. There was too great a possibility that Garth had assigned private investigators to keep tabs on all his top people. He's done it before when he's been nervous about security."

"But the party was neutral ground," Shannon interposed grimly.

"Exactly. The party was the safest opportunity I was going to get and I knew it. I took the one copy of the bid package I had managed to make."

Shannon eyed him. "How did you make that one copy? I thought Garth kept track of every piece of paper relating to that bid that came out of Bonnie's typewriter."

"There are limits to what any man can do in the way of security measures." Wes smiled. "And I had some inside help."

"Bonnie." Shannon took a deep breath and expelled it slowly.

"Bonnie thinks she's in love with me. Women in love will do strange things."

"It's incredible. Everyone around Garth was plotting against him."

"Including you," Wes snapped.

Shannon ignored that. "All right, you managed to make one copy of the document. Why didn't you make two or three copies?"

"Are you kidding? And risk having some investigator find it in my possession?" Wes shook his head at her dumb question. "Even having one copy on me for a few hours made me very nervous. I hadn't realized how tense this sort of thing makes a man. Besides, I didn't get the copy until the last minute. Bonnie was willing but not terribly clever. She finally got it made for me the day of the party. Right around lunchtime."

Shannon's eyes widened. "Oh, my God."

"That's right. If it hadn't been for your little diversion that day, Bonnie might not have had a free moment to take the bid down to a copying machine and run it. But when you showed up, Garth seemed to forget all about his normal paranoia. He was concentrating on you so much, he didn't bother to pick up the bid papers and put them in his briefcase before he took you to lunch. He just locked his office door. Bonnie has a key to that. She and I just waited until you left the building and then we went back inside, hoping Sheridan had been careless. Sure enough, all the papers were lying there on the desk, just as we'd left them. She grabbed the bid and ran it off while I kept an eye out for Garth's return. I don't mind telling you, I was getting a little nervous. I had wanted to transfer it that night and time was running out."

"The night of the party," Shannon began slowly, "how did the bid document get into my tote? Did you mistake it for Bonnie's?"

Wes's mouth twisted savagely. "I had the bid inside my jacket when I arrived. I had a hunch Bonnie would draw the line at being the agent I needed. She was too scared. She'd been reluctant to go as far as she had and I wasn't sure how much farther I could push her. So I told her I would take care of the final transfer to Kenyon. After I'd been at the party a while I told Kenyon he could pick up the bid inside the tote bag with the crazy design on the side. Then I wandered down the hall to the bedroom and slipped the thing inside the only tote that was on the bed."

"But there were two totes," Shannon argued. "Mine and Bonnie's."

"Not when I slipped into the bedroom," Wes gritted savagely. "I found out later that Bonnie had taken hers into the powder room for a few minutes. They both looked alike to me when I saw them earlier in the office. Since Bonnie had made a point of leaving hers in the bedroom, I assumed the one that was on the bed was hers. At any rate, I put the bid package in the one tote bag I found and left."

"Kenyon was supposed to wander in later and retrieve it. But Kenyon made the mistake of making a pass at me en route."

Wes nodded. "Garth saw him and went into his 'hands off my woman' routine. After which he apparently sent you into the bedroom to grab your purse because he was dragging you home early."

"So that's how I wound up with the document in my tote," Shannon muttered.

"After which, you were smart enough to take advantage of a real windfall, weren't you?" Wes looked thoroughly disgusted. "Hell, I made it easy for you, didn't I? I don't know what your original plan was, but when you found the bid in your tote, you could afford to abandon whatever complicated plan you originally had in mind when you seduced Sheridan. Life had suddenly gotten much simpler. But I'll tell you something, Shannon. You've made a serious mistake by continuing the affair with Sheridan. If you had any sense, you'd have transferred the bid to your client and gotten safely out of Garth's way. When he finds out what you've done, you won't stand a chance. He won't let another woman get away with betraying him. Believe me."

"Garth knows I didn't steal that bid package."

Wes cocked one brow. "Just because you played innocent and called the cops last night? I wouldn't count on it. Sheridan's been acting a little strangely for the past few months but no one claims he's come down with a bad case of the stupids. That guard he had assigned to watch your cottage was probably meant as much to keep an eye on your activities as it was to protect you. Sheridan doesn't take chances."

"You're crazy."

"No, but I am getting anxious. Time is running out. You and I have to talk business. Have you handed the bid over to your client?"

"I haven't handed it over to anyone!"

"Good. I figured that if you had already made the transfer, you might have been dumb enough to keep a copy. I was willing to buy a second copy from you if that's all that's left. Kenyon doesn't need to know someone else has also paid for and gotten the information. But it's safer for both of us if you've still got the one I brought to the party. How much do you want for it, Shannon?"

"Not one thin dime, you fool. I'm not selling it to you," she snapped.

"I must have it, Shannon. You don't know Kenyon."

"What can he do to you that's any worse than what Garth will do when he finds out what's happened?" Shannon taunted.

"Kenyon's promised me a job running his new R & D branch in Tucson. He's going places and he's going to take me with him. It's become obvious to me during the past year that Sheridan isn't going to keep expanding. I think he's getting tired of the business. I don't want to hang around with a firm that's starting to go soft. But between the two of them, Sheridan and Kenyon can ruin me. I need Kenyon to protect me from Garth if and when he finds out what happened. I want to be safely on Kenyon's payroll and out of the state when the time comes."

"But if you don't deliver to Kenyon he'll turn his back on you. Then you'll be caught between a rock and a hard place, won't you? Garth will have his revenge and you won't have anyone to protect you from him. You'll be lucky to get another job in the field."

"You've got it. So now you must see why I'm willing to talk business. Name your price, Shannon. It'll be much safer for you to make the deal this way rather than trying to cut your own."

"No."

"Don't be a fool," Wes exploded. "You're nothing but a two-bit hustler who's trying to cash in on a lucky break. Don't think you can go up against me and get away with it. I want that bid. I'll take it the hard way if you won't sell it to me."

"You tried taking it the hard way last night," Shannon pointed out. "It didn't work."

Wes reached out and grabbed her arm. "Come on. We're going back to the cottage. I'm not leaving until I have that bid."

"I haven't got it," Shannon said with a calm she was far from feeling. "Garth took it with him this morning."

"The hell he did. How would he know you've got it? You sure wouldn't have told him. I'll bet when you called the cops last night you made up some line about a prowler without bothering to explain just what that prowler really wanted. Now move!"

Wes jerked her forward, causing her to stumble. Shannon started to struggle but this time her opponent was ready for her. She found her arm twisted painfully behind her back. Without another word, Wes shoved her toward the cliff.

Shannon began to climb reluctantly, her arm aching from the grip Wes had on it. She could only hope that Ted Walters had returned from lunch.

GARTH HAD BEEN on the road an hour when he decided to make the call to his office. He picked up the phone and spoke crisply to the mobile operator. His mind had been running in high gear ever since he had left Shannon, and he didn't like the various directions his thoughts kept taking. The need to get the situation under control was gnawing at him, and he became increasingly impatient with the long drive. Briefly he considered driving as far as Santa Rosa and chartering a plane back to San Jose. But common sense said that by the time he could make the arrangements and get from the airport to his office, he would have chewed up nearly as much time as the drive would.

He should have pushed that locksmith, Garth thought while he waited for his call to go through. He should have insisted Shannon's locks be installed several days ago. Maybe the intruder would never have gotten inside the cottage if there had been decent locks on the door.

But perhaps good security wouldn't have helped at all, he decided. The guy might have simply waited outside the cottage and grabbed Shannon when she opened her door.

The only thing that might have deterred the intruder would have been Garth's presence. And Garth had been two hundred miles away when Shannon had needed him. The memory made his fingers clamp more fiercely around the phone as Bonnie came on the line.

"Mr. Sheridan, I've been wondering where you were," Bonnie said in her smooth, professional voice. "I couldn't find any messages saying you'd be late in to work, and I was beginning to be concerned."

It crossed Garth's mind that the concern in his secretary's voice was slightly more than he would have expected from Bonnie Garnett. He dismissed the thought. "I'm calling from the car. Put me through to Wes."

There was a short pause and then Bonnie said politely, "I'm afraid Mr. McIntyre isn't in yet, either. I was informed he had a breakfast meeting with Mr.

Jensen of TechHi. I think he expects the meeting to take all morning."

"Damn." Garth swallowed the rest of the curse and told Bonnie goodbye rather abruptly.

"But when shall I expect you, Mr. Sheridan?"

"In a couple of hours."

That seemed to startle her. "A couple of hours? You're not just driving across town?"

"I'm on my way back from the coast."

There was another pause from Bonnie. "I see. I hadn't realized." She took a breath and said, "Then we'll see you in a couple of hours. Goodbye, Mr. Sheridan." She hung up the phone.

Garth drove another couple of miles, turning everything over in his mind, including Bonnie's unexpected concern for his late arrival at the office. Something was very wrong, and the root lay somewhere close to the office of the president of Sherilectronics. He knew it. He also knew the feeling of being on the wrong end of an act of betrayal.

On a hunch, Garth picked up his phone again and asked for information. A moment later the operator put him through to Matt Jensen's office at TechHi.

"I'm sorry, Mr. Jensen is in a meeting and can't be disturbed," Jensen's secretary announced. "May I take a message?"

"Jensen's in a meeting with McIntyre who works for me. I'm Sheridan," Garth said impatiently. "It's Wes

McIntyre I need to reach. Do you know where they're having breakfast?"

"Oh, but they're not having breakfast, sir." The secretary sounded startled at his assumption. "Mr. Jensen is in a meeting with his accountant. I haven't seen Mr. McIntyre."

Garth took his foot off the accelerator as a cold chill of premonition went through him. "I see. Thanks for the information. Must be my mistake."

He hung up and slammed the Porsche to a halt at the side of the highway. Then he sat behind the wheel, drumming his fingers on the leather and marshaled his thoughts once more.

McIntyre. The man he thought he knew so well because Wes's mind worked the same as his own. But for the past few months Garth's own mind had been working a little differently than usual.

Garth asked the mobile operator to put through one more call. When the head of Balley Security came on the line, Garth didn't bother with the preliminaries.

"I want your man to keep his eye out for a guy named Wes McIntyre. I have a hunch he's involved in this mess." Quickly Garth launched into a description. Halfway through it, he was interrupted.

"But, Mr. Sheridan, you had Walters pulled off that detail over an hour ago. I have a record of your call."

"The hell I did," Garth breathed, aware of a tightening in his stomach. "I didn't make any call, George."

"Just a second. Here's the note from my secretary. The call came in at ten thirty-five. You specifically left word that everything was under control, and you didn't want to pay for any more of Walters's time."

"You didn't take the call yourself?"

"No, I was in a meeting."

"It was a phony, George," Garth said bluntly. "Get Walters back out to that cottage. Now."

It was the other man's turn to swear. "I'm sorry, Garth. But it's going to take him some time to get back there. I'll start him moving as fast as I can."

"You do that," Garth said savagely, putting the Porsche into gear and spinning the sleek car back onto the highway. "I'm going back myself. This whole thing has turned to fertilizer." *And it's my own damn fault,* he added silently as he opened up the Porsche.

A weekend lover wasn't of much use to his woman. He was doomed to always be in the wrong place when she needed him.

WHEN WES SHOVED HER through the kitchen door of her cottage, Shannon gave up any hope of being spotted by the security guard from Balley. Even if he had returned from lunch, he wouldn't be expecting an approach from the back of the house. From his position on the opposite side of the road, Ted Walters wouldn't be able to see what was happening at the kitchen door. Shannon told herself she was going to have to think of something else.

Her arm was aching from the fierce pressure Wes had on it. She had taken him by surprise last night, but today he seemed to be waiting for her to try something. Without the element of surprise, she didn't stand much of a chance. McIntyre was a good deal larger and stronger than Shannon was. She stumbled as she was pushed through the back door.

"This is all a waste of time, you know," she tried to say calmly as she caught herself on the edge of the table.

"Is it?" Wes asked contemptuously. "I don't think so. I think if we look real hard around here we'll come up with another copy of that Carstairs bid. Find it!"

Shannon tried to free herself once more, twisting angrily in McIntyre's grasp even as he tightened his hold. Desperately she looked around, seeking an object she could use in her own defense. Her eyes lighted on the teakettle sitting on the stove, and she was wondering if she could get hold of it when everything in the kitchen suddenly went still, including Wes McIntyre.

"Sheridan." Wes sounded dazed. He didn't release Shannon, but his eyes were fixed on the doorway into the living room. "What the hell are you doing here? You're supposed to be halfway back to San Jose. I watched you leave myself."

Shannon's head came up with a quick movement, her eyes widening in relief. "Garth! Oh, Garth, thank heavens you're here!" He was standing like a rock in the doorway, his eyes colder than Shannon had ever seen them. In one hand he held the copy of the bid he had taken with him earlier.

"Let her go." The words were far too quiet. Garth looked at Wes.

"Listen to me, Sheridan, don't be a fool. The woman's been putting you through the hoop for weeks. She's the one responsible for the theft of that bid. She's been working with Bonnie. I just found out myself what was going on. The two of them have been running rings around both of us. I finally realized what was happening when I—"

"Let her go."

Abruptly Shannon felt her arm being freed. She didn't hesitate. Running across the kitchen, she hurled herself against Garth. His arm went around her as she buried her face in his chest.

"Don't listen to him, Garth. He's the one behind this whole thing. He and Bonnie copied the bid that day we went to lunch in San Jose. He screwed up that night at the party and put the bid into my tote instead of Bonnie's. Kenyon was supposed to retrieve it later, but we left early and the bid was already inside my bag. That's why I—"

"You going to let another woman make a fool out of you, Garth?" Wes asked with soft contempt. "I thought you learned your lesson after Christine left."

Shannon clung more tightly, a new kind of fear replacing the sort she had been experiencing around Wes. "Garth, no, please. Don't listen to him."

Garth very gently unwound her arms from around his waist. Without glancing down at her, he set her aside. Shannon stood paralyzed in the doorway as Garth took a few steps into the kitchen to confront Wes McIntyre.

"What was Kenyon offering, Wes? More money? A better job? Stock in the company?" Garth sounded as if he were only remotely interested.

"Ask her," Wes snarled, gesturing toward Shannon. "She's the one who tried to sell you out. Ask her what he was offering."

Garth ignored him. "You must have known that sooner or later I'd figure out who'd sold Kenyon the copy of the bid. And you know me well enough to realize I wouldn't have just written the whole thing off to experience. I would have come after you. So Kenyon must have found a way to convince you he could protect you."

"You're trying to blame me, Sheridan, because you don't want to admit you let another woman get past your defenses again." Wes was suddenly calm and controlled. He glanced at Shannon. "She's all right, I suppose, but nothing spectacular. Bonnie would have been a better bet. You could have had her, instead, I think. But with Bonnie you were always strictly business."

"Is that why she turned to you so easily?"

Wes lifted one shoulder negligently. "You should be grateful. If I hadn't been sleeping with your secretary, Garth, I probably wouldn't have figured out what was going on here. But Bonnie talks a little too much in the sack. She'd given up on getting your attention, but she hadn't given up on getting even for the fact that you managed to ignore her for damn near five years. So she worked out a plan. But she needed an assistant. Someone who might be able to get close to you. She went into partnership with her good friend Shannon Raine. Fed her the information Shannon needed about your trip to the coast, made sure she knew about the party and all the other details. Then they contacted Ed Kenyon."

"He's lying, Garth," Shannon said quietly.

"I know," Garth stated.

"Who are you going to trust, Sheridan? The guy who's been with you for over three years or that little hustler? I'm the one who helped you bring off the Kilton deal, remember? I'm the one who worked out the logistics on the Barton order. Hell, there have been more times than I can count that you've relied on me and I've always come through, haven't I? How long have you known her? Two or three weeks at the most. You know something? I could never understand how a sharp guy like you let that wife of yours pull that stunt a few years back, but now I guess I've figured it out. You're a sucker for a certain kind of woman, aren't you, Sheridan?"

"The mistake I made this time around was in trusting you, Wes. I should have seen the signs and realized you were getting restless. God knows I've seen them in others. But either I haven't been concentrating on my business as much as I should have during the past few months or I've just gotten damn tired of distrusting everyone on my payroll. Did you know it gets to be something of a strain, Wes? Not being able to trust anyone, I mean. A year ago I would have kept a closer eye on you. A year ago you'd never have gotten as far as getting that copy of the bid from Bonnie. I would have sensed something was going on and done something about it sooner. But I've changed during the past year, Wes. And keeping tabs on everyone isn't worth the effort anymore. It takes energy. It wears you out. And it limits you in a way I hadn't quite understood until I met Shannon."

"You're telling me you're too tired to exercise a little caution around a bitch like her?" Wes shouted incredulously.

"You're missing the point, but I suppose it doesn't matter. Why don't we call a halt to the discussion. I'm sure you don't want to hear that I'm making new plans for my life, and I sure as hell don't want to hear any more of your idiotic accusations and excuses."

"You bastard!" Wes exploded. He launched himself toward Garth, fury and desperation suddenly in his eyes. Garth shifted slightly, depriving Wes of his target. The younger man ended up against the kitchen wall, the impact knocking one of Shannon's framed silk-screen prints to the floor.

"Damn you, Sheridan." Wes struggled to regain his balance, his face locked in a snarl of rage. He swung one arm wildly.

Garth stepped aside and caught McIntyre on the jaw with a fist that carried the full force of his upper body. Wes staggered back against the wall and slid slowly to the floor, his eyes glazed, although he was not unconscious.

Garth stood watching him for a few seconds. "There are still a few things you're going to have to learn if you expect to survive in the jungle, Wes. One of them is that sometimes the business gets downright physical. If you're going to spend the rest of your career stealing other people's secrets and betraying their trust, you'd better expect things to get rough on occasion. That, by the way, was for manhandling Shannon, not for trying to cheat me."

"I never touched her." Wes's voice was strained as he put the back of his hand to his mouth. There was a trace of blood on his lips.

Wordlessly Garth stepped closer and yanked at the front of Wes's shirt. The fabric tore effortlessly. Garth pushed it back until Wes's bandaged arm was clearly visible. "She used a knife on you last time, Wes. No telling what she would have come up with this time. You should be glad I was here."

"The bitch."

"The lady saved Sherilectronics from being screwed by the one man its president was stupid enough to trust. I thought I knew you, Wes. Thought I understood how your mind worked. You always had the makings of a bastard, but I assumed I was paying enough to make sure you were my bastard. What did Kenyon offer?"

Wes stared at him sullenly. "Go to hell."

"How much did he offer? What's the going rate these days for a man's loyalty?"

Wes's eyes were slitted with resentment. "A future. For the past year I've been getting the impression there isn't going to be one at Sherilectronics. Not an important one, at any rate. When I first came to work for you the sky was the limit. You were the most aggressive SOB in the Valley and you were going places. I knew someone like you could take me along for the ride. But this past year everything changed, didn't it,

Garth? You've lost your appetite for the business. Oh, sure, the company is still in good shape and this Carstairs job will be a real coup if you land it, but something's changed. You didn't seem to want to dominate the market any longer. You were getting soft. I decided I'd better get out while the getting was good. Damned if I was going to go down in a sinking ship."

"And Kenyon's ship looked more watertight?"

"He's going to be number one on the West Coast soon. The top slot could have belonged to Sherilectronics if you hadn't started losing your taste for that kind of warfare."

Garth studied him. "One of the reasons I hired you, Wes, was that you struck me as being reasonably perceptive. I was right. Unfortunately, you aren't so bright in other ways. You should never have used Shannon. You should have been perceptive enough to realize she was definitely off limits. Maybe if you'd kept her out of it, I might have taken care of you the usual way. You'd have been fired and you might have had a tough time getting another job, but you'd probably have been able to dig up something. You're sharp and you're slick. But you involved Shannon. Don't expect to get away with that sort of stupidity."

"It's her own fault." Wes groaned, touching his jaw. "God knows I didn't want to get anyone else involved. Having to use Bonnie was risky enough. But that night at the party when I realized Shannon had taken the bid home in that damn tote bag, I figured I didn't have any choice. She had to be working her own game. It was the only thing that made sense. I came after her, hoping I'd find she still had the bid or a copy of it. There was a good chance she would have been stupid enough to make a second copy before selling one to her client. She wasn't a pro. Just an opportunist."

"Your basic mistake was in assuming everyone else was as ambitious as you are, McIntyre."

"She's as guilty as I am, Sheridan. If you don't see that, you're blind. She's been using you."

Shannon shivered. It was clear that as long as he was going down, Wes intended to try dragging her with him. She said nothing, waiting for Garth to make his decision. He didn't even glance at her.

"Call the cops, Shannon."

Wes's head snapped around. "What charge?"

"How about something along the lines of breaking and entering? That wound in your shoulder is going to be an interesting bit of evidence. Then there's your assault on Shannon today. I witnessed it, don't forget. And last but not least, we'll come up with some sort of charge to cover your attempt at industrial espionage."

"Nothing came out of that," Wes protested. "You can't prove a damn thing."

"I can make sure you have a tough time ever getting a decent job again. You'd better believe Kenyon is going to play innocent. He won't touch you with a ten-foot pole now. You know that as well as I do. And if you ever go near Shannon again, I won't go through the formalities of calling the cops. I'll take care of you myself. You've worked with me long enough to know I mean what I say, haven't you, Wes?" Garth didn't wait for an answer. He flicked another glance at Shannon. "Go ahead. Make the call."

IT WAS A LONG TIME LATER before Shannon found herself alone with Garth. He had spent a great deal of time with the local authorities. Wes was in custody, although how long that would last was anyone's guess. He was already on the phone to his lawyer. Regardless of the outcome, Shannon was fairly certain McIntyre would be staying out of her way. She had seen the expression in his eyes when Garth had warned him.

Garth had been very subdued since returning from the offices of the town's tiny police department. He hadn't said a word when he'd walked in the front door. Instead he'd gone immediately to the phone and placed a call to his own office at Sherilectronics. When there was no answer, he'd hung up and redialed.

"Miss Graham? Do me a favor and send someone to cover Bonnie's desk, will you? She's taken emergency leave, apparently. I'm out of town. We'll arrange something more permanent when I get back." There was a pause while Garth listened to the voice on the other end of the line. Then he said, "No, I don't think Bonnie will be returning. Thank you, Miss Graham." He hung up the phone and walked thoughtfully over to the kitchen doorway. He stood watching Shannon as she concentrated on spreading peanut butter on crackers.

Shannon felt the quiet gaze on her, but she didn't look at Garth. The tension that had been tightening her nerves all day was still in effect. She couldn't seem to relax even though the action was apparently over. She had started work on the peanut butter and crackers in the hopes that food would do the trick.

"Bonnie's disappeared?" she ventured.

"She probably got scared when I called in asking for Wes. Since she had an alibi for him, she must have known where he was. My guess is she checked and found out I'd called Jensen's firm to try to get hold of Wes. When she found out I must have discovered he had no meeting with Jensen she probably panicked. Add the fact that I wasn't in San Jose but returning from the coast, and she had a good reason to panic. She must have decided things were deteriorating rapidly and done what any smart person would have done under the circumstances."

"Run?"

"Uh-huh."

"I can't say I blame her," Shannon said quietly. "Are you going to track her down and bring charges?"

"Do you think I should bother?"

"No," Shannon murmured. "She got talked into something she shouldn't have, but I have a feeling she'll have learned her lesson."

Garth's mouth curved in a faint, cynical smile. "Like hell. She had a close call, but if she gets away with it, she'll probably try it again on some other unsuspecting employer. You have a very rosy picture of human nature, honey."

"I liked her, Garth."

He shrugged. "So did I. Damn good secretary. But I think I'll take your advice and forget her. Let the next dumb employer deal with her. Besides, she'll be a good, walking advertisement for your totes. She always did have a sense of style."

Shannon slid him a sidelong glance, unsure if he was making a joke or not. Garth's sense of humor was sometimes rather limited and sometimes rather odd, she had discovered. "I can understand how she must have felt all those years during which you never bothered to notice her as a woman," she declared vehemently. "I would have been desperate, too, under the circumstances."

Garth's smile flickered momentarily into a full grin. "But unlike Bonnie, you took the positive, straightforward, honest approach. Sometimes I think that's the only kind of approach you can take. It's one of the reasons I worried about you so much. The rest of the world doesn't always operate the way you do. Were you afraid I'd believe Wes's lies there at the end?" he added quietly.

"I wasn't sure," Shannon admitted, the words halting. "He's been with you a long time. You seemed to trust him. You've only known me a few weeks."

"I've never believed you were involved in the theft, Shannon."

She looked up at him finally, her eyes full of the uncertainty she was feeling. "Because you're a logical kind of man and you realize how unlikely it was that I was a thief? Or because you still think I'm too naive to plan such a clever operation? Why, Garth? Why didn't you believe what Wes implied?"

Garth gazed at her pensively for a long while before saying simply, "I didn't choose to believe him because I love you, Shannon."

The answer caught her by surprise. It wasn't at all what she was expecting. Shannon dropped the knife she had been using to spread peanut butter and stood staring, openmouthed, for a full ten seconds. "Oh, Garth," she breathed and the spell broke as she went into his arms. "I love you so much, and I was so afraid you wouldn't be able to really love me in return."

His arms closed around her with an urgency that told its own story. "It took me a while to realize what was happening," Garth whispered into her hair. "At first, I was sure you were just looking for a quick fling. I wanted you, but I intended to keep things on my terms. Then I began to realize you were sincere and I knew I was falling for you. When I decided I wanted a full-blown affair I suspected I was in love, but it seemed safer not to admit it. But I wanted to keep you safe. I wanted to keep you out of my world because my world isn't very pleasant."

"You wanted me to be waiting for you on the weekends. You were afraid I'd get contaminated if I moved into your life completely, weren't you, Garth?"

"Not exactly. I trusted you. But you seemed so soft and . . . and innocent in so many ways. I was afraid you'd get chewed up alive by people like Ed Kenyon and the others at that party. I knew from firsthand experience you're a little reckless when it comes to trusting strangers."

"You were the only stranger I was ever really reckless with," she protested.

"Maybe. But you did seem a little unworldly at times. A little naive. I wanted to protect you. But there was a selfish side to that protection. I'm just beginning to understand it. The truth was, I didn't want you to see my working world. I think, deep down, I was afraid you would hate it and, sooner or later, come to hate me. My world is so different from yours, so much harsher. How could a soft, sweet, gentle artist from the coast ever approve of either me or my other life? I was protecting myself rather than you."

"I think," Shannon said slowly, "that the reason you were afraid I'd hate your world was because you, yourself, have come to hate it."

There was a stillness in Garth that alarmed Shannon. She lifted her head from his shoulder to meet his eyes.

Garth's fingers moved in slow circles on Shannon's shoulders as he gazed down at her. "You may be right," he finally said. "McIntyre really is quite shrewd in some ways, you know. What he said earlier about my having lost the taste for the kind of infighting it takes to survive and flourish in Silicon Valley was damn close to the truth. One of the reasons I wanted that Carstairs job so badly was to prove to myself that I could still hold my own. But during the past few days I've realized getting that job will do something much more important. It will make Sherilectronics look very, very good to a potential buyer. And I'm going to start looking for a buyer right away, Shannon."

"Why?"

"For the past six or eight months I've been realizing I wanted to make a change. Now I know just what kind of change. I want to sell out."

"Sell out! But, Garth, you've built that company up from scratch. It's a huge chunk of your life."

"My past life. Shannon, everything crystallized for me this morning when I found out Wes had called Balley and pretended he was me so he could get Walters taken off guard duty. I felt so damn helpless when I realized how far away I was and that you had no one to protect you. Just as helpless as I felt when I learned an intruder had gotten into your cottage. In both cases the reason you were in jeopardy was because of me. Weekend lovers aren't very useful. Weekend husbands wouldn't be much better. Annie was right. I couldn't even protect you from the dangers I had brought into your life, let alone fix the plumbing, make hot soup for you when you get sick or keep your car in good working condition. I want to be with you on a full-time basis. I want a real marriage, not a weekend retreat. And I want to get out of a world I don't much like anymore."

"What will you do, Garth?" Shannon smiled mistily. "Write poetry, after all? Maybe the great American novel?"

He grinned faintly. "No amount of imagination on your part is going to make me into a poet or a writer, honey. But I do know something about business, specifically the electronics business. I intend to stay out of the rat race of Silicon Valley, but there are other ways to make a living with electronics. I've been thinking about starting up a small consulting firm. But I definitely wouldn't establish it in San Jose."

Shannon hugged him. "Where would you establish it?"

"That's something you and I will have to discuss." Garth's eyes became more serious for a moment. "This part of the coast is a little too isolated for even a small company such as the one I'm planning. Would you mind very much if we moved to Santa Barbara or Ventura? I know you've made your home here and you have friends and I know I have no right to ask you to change your life for me."

"You're changing your life for me, aren't you?"

"For both of us," he said firmly.

"Well, I'm more than willing to make a change for both of us, too. No, Garth, I don't mind moving. Santa Barbara or Ventura sounds wonderful."

"Shannon, I love you." He cradled her face between his hands. "I've never loved like this before in my life. Maybe that's why I was so cautious with you.

I knew I had something special, and I was terrified of losing it."

"You won't lose me by loving me," Shannon assured him as she wrapped her arms around his neck. "And I appreciate your desire to protect me. After all, I feel the same way about you. But I do wish you wouldn't think of me as so unsophisticated and unworldly that I need to be shielded as if were a silly, scatterbrained artist. I'm an adult and I'm not helpless, despite current evidence to the contrary. I don't need to be kept in cotton wool."

He groaned, holding her close. "Be patient with me, sweetheart. My instincts are pretty strong where you're concerned. The need to protect you is one of those instincts. I'll try to be reasonable."

"And when you're not being reasonable?" she teased gently.

"Then I suspect you'll let me know it."

"Umm. I see some trouble ahead," she murmured.

"A few marital squabbles are only to be expected."

Shannon laughed. "You sound very philosophical about marriage, all of a sudden."

"I'm a believer in marriage under certain circumstances. Have you forgotten that lecture I tried to give Annie and Dan the night you invited me to dinner?"

"I'll never forget," Shannon said in heartfelt tones. "I almost wrote you off as a complete and utter social disaster that night."

"But instead you gave me another chance." He spoke with supreme male satisfaction.

"I couldn't help myself. From the beginning I've had this incredible compulsion to get to know you. Every time I told myself I should just give up the whole project, I'd find myself pushing again, trying to get closer to you. And after I'd realized I was in love with you..."

. "Speaking of which, you are going to marry me, aren't you?" He looked down at her intently.

"Yes, Garth."

"I don't really think of you as helpless or incompetent, you know," he added softly. "If I ever had any illusions on that score you cleared them up last night when you managed to fight off an intruder and rescue that damn bid package!"

"That impressed you, huh?"

"I'll say. I hope to hell you don't have to impress me like that again."

"I hated having that stupid bid package in the house, but I realized you'd left it with me to prove something. I couldn't let Wes or anyone else have it, Garth. It was a symbol of the fact that you trusted me. And I was responsible for it."

"You could have saved yourself a lot of grief by simply handing it over to Wes that night."

Shannon shook her head. "Impossible. There was no way I would have willingly done that."

He tightened his hold on her. "I know. I'll always trust you, Shannon. No matter what happens. You're the one person in the world I believe in. I need you to believe in me."

"I do."

"Just promise me you won't get yourself in any more situations in which you're required to go to such dramatic lengths to impress me with your valor and dedication," Garth said, smiling. "I don't think my aging constitution will stand the shock another time."

"I'd much rather impress you in other ways." Shannon's eyes shimmered with love as she looked up at him. "I love you so much, Garth." She tightened her arms around him, pressing close to the warmth and strength he offered, giving him her own feminine version of the same things.

"What about the peanut-butter crackers?" he asked, his voice tinged with sensual amusement.

"They'll keep."

"I'm glad they will," Garth said as he lifted her into his arms. "Because it's becoming obvious that I won't. Not for much longer. You have a profound effect upon me, honey. I don't know whatever made me think I could get through five days a week without having you in my bed."

Garth carried her down the hall to the bedroom and settled Shannon in the center of the bed. Then he came down beside her and slid his hand under the collar of her shirt. "Love me, Shannon. Whatever happens, don't stop loving me. I need you so much."

"It works both ways," she whispered, drawing his mouth down to within an inch of hers. "I need you, too. And I'll never stop loving you. You may be destined to make your living as a businessman, but I've got news for you, Garth Sheridan. I was right the first time I saw you. You have the soul of an impassioned poet."

"Is that right?" He began undoing the buttons of her shirt.

"Oh, yes," she assured him. "It takes one artsy type to recognize another, you know."

"Maybe that's why I couldn't resist you, right from the start. We're soul mates."

"Exactly."

His mouth closed over hers, and Shannon surrendered to the passion and the love that she knew would always exist between herself and Garth. Just before the mounting excitement captured her completely, she mentally sketched two fancifully decorated initials, an S and a G. They would be done in the Carolingian style with beautiful birds and shimmering dragons woven around them.

Then there was no other reality but the heated fire of their mutual love. Shannon touched her lover with wonder, reveling in the aggressive power of his masculinity. It was such a perfect complement to her own, very female power. She and Garth flowed together the way her intricate designs did, capturing and releasing, intertwining and shifting, spiraling and dancing. In the dark shadows of the bed a jeweled dragon chased a fairy queen and then changed into a great soaring bird that flew after a brilliantly hued butterfly. Over and around the two went, tasting each other's fiery passion, coupling and uncoupling, teasing and promising until at last the whole, beautiful picture was complete, an illuminated image of perfect harmony and pleasure.

As she clung to Garth in the aftermath of their lovemaking, the image of the silk-screen design Shannon had been mentally sketching returned. Before it slipped away again Shannon studied it and knew the initials would not stand alone. They would be linked together, intertwined completely just as she was forever linked to Garth.

Epilogue

THE ANNOUNCEMENT that Sherilectronics had won the Carstairs contract came on the same day that Shannon and Garth were married. Annie O'Connor Turcott insisted on preparing the wedding feast for the small group of guests, and Dan took Garth aside to give him some advice on the fine points of being a husband. Having been one for more than two weeks himself, Dan felt obligated to pass along the masculine wisdom of the ages. He accompanied his lecture with a great deal of champagne.

Shannon had watched in amusement as the two men stood talking earnestly together in Annie's fragrant kitchen.

"I think they're both going to take to their husbandly duties the way ducks take to water," Annie murmured in Shannon's ear as she followed the line of her friend's gaze.

"Amazing how adaptable the male of the species can be," Shannon responded with a grin as she sipped her champagne.

"Uh-huh. Somehow I was always fairly certain Garth would marry you. The man would never have any peace of mind if he didn't. He needs you for that, you know."

"Peace of mind?"

"Umm. You're the one who can keep that fascinating dark, brooding quality at bay. It's a part of him. It goes deep. You were right about him having the soul of a poet somewhere inside that businessman's body. With you around it won't take over his life. I rather think he was falling prey to it before you arrived and took him in hand."

"Nice to know I'm useful," Shannon remarked.

"Oh, you'll find Garth useful, too."

"Yes, I know. He's going to take very good care of me." There was amusement in Shannon's voice.

"Don't knock it," her friend advised. "Being useful to each other is part of being married."

"I can't imagine where you and Dan picked up all this insight into marriage so suddenly."

"Comes naturally," Annie assured her. "Wait and see."

"Does Dan fuss about everything from the locks on the doors to the kind of car you're allowed to drive?"

"Sure. But I'll be the first to admit I tend to fuss about how much coffee he drinks when he's writing and how he shouldn't lift the garbage sacks the way he does with his bad back."

"I guess it works both ways," Shannon mused complacently. Now that she and Garth would be sharing their lives completely, she thought she could take his tendency toward overprotectiveness in stride.

"Garth seems a lot more interested in his wedding than he does in the fact that his company got that bid, by the way," Annie commented, glancing at where the groom stood talking so seriously to Dan.

"The Carstairs bid was just a stepping-stone to smaller and more important things," Shannon said. "Much more important things." Her eyes filled with love as she excused herself and went to join her husband. Garth waited for her across the room, his crystal gaze alive with the fierce emotion he felt toward his wife.

"I am now an expert on marriage," he warned her with a promising grin.

"Is that right? Taking lessons from the expert?" Shannon smiled at Dan.

"That's right," Dan assured her grandly. "I was just telling Garth that he shouldn't wait to start a family. He's going to be forty in a couple of years and you're nearly thirty. I think the two of you should hop to it without any unnecessary delay. Nothing like a family to settle a man down."

Shannon was about to make a pithy reply to that when she was interrupted by a loud, strident voice behind her. Turning, she took in the sight of the red-headed apparition dressed in black and red. Only Verna Montana would wear black and red to a wedding. Her hair, a little too red to be natural, was a cloud of wild curls that framed the thin, elfin features of her face. She was fifty going on thirty, and she had indulged herself in a fair amount of champagne.

"A firm hand on the reins is what it takes to settle a man down," she declared in ringing tones. "Handle him the way Kate handled Petruchio, Shannon, and you'll do fine. Good move getting him to marry you, by the way. Enormously clever. But it's only a first step. You can't let up now or he's liable to run loose again."

Garth looked at the woman. "Do we know this lady, Shannon?"

"This," Shannon announced, "is Verna Montana."

"The perpetrator of that fiasco masquerading as a modern-day version of *The Taming of the Shrew*?"

"One and the same," Shannon admitted, wondering if Garth was about to revert to his antisocial ways.

"My *Shrew* was a brilliant departure from the usual male-biased version," Verna said grandly.

"Your *Shrew* was an abomination. A total hash. Absolutely idiotic."

Shannon groaned and looked to Dan for support. Dan lifted one shoulder helplessly.

"You obviously have no understanding of the art of the theater or the importance of interpretation when dealing with the classics," Verna informed Garth.

"That's probably true," he agreed. "But as it happens, I owe you a profound debt of gratitude, Ms. Montana."

Verna blinked in astonishment, clearly halted at the beginning of the lecture she had been about to deliver. "You do?"

Garth reached out and took Shannon's arm, folding it possessively against his side. "The night I saw your version of the *Shrew* was the night I first—"

Shannon rushed to cut him off, remembering in horror what had actually happened that night after the play. "Garth, don't you dare say it. Not in public. I would never forgive you!"

"It was the night," he continued relentlessly, "that I first realized I was falling in love with Shannon."

Shannon lifted her eyes skyward in relief. She had been afraid he was about to say something far more embarrassing. From the look in his eyes, she could tell he was definitely thinking of that night in far more earthy terms.

"Ready to leave, sweetheart?" he asked blandly as Verna beamed.

"Definitely."

"Then let's get going. I think it's time we were on our way."

"Before you say something you shouldn't?" she whispered as they began saying goodbye to their guests.

"I'm reformed," he told her. "The perfect party guest."

"Fat chance."

"You're looking at a new me."

"Pity. There were several things about the old you that I rather liked."

"Well, you're in luck. Some things never change." He swept her out the door, laughter and passion and love in his eyes.

Shannon's expression echoed his. They would build their future together, a future that would bind them as inextricably as the letters S and G on the framed silk-screen print that was waiting back in Shannon's cottage.

THREE UNFORGETTABLE HEROINES
THREE AWARD-WINNING AUTHORS

Untamed

MAVERICK HEARTS

A unique collection of historical short stories that capture the spirit of America's last frontier.

HEATHER GRAHAM POZZESSERE—over 10 million copies of her books in print worldwide
Lonesome Rider—The story of an Eastern widow and the renegade half-breed who becomes her protector.

PATRICIA POTTER—an author whose books are consistently Waldenbooks bestsellers
Against the Wind—Two people, battered by heartache, prove that love can heal all.

JOAN JOHNSTON—award-winning Western historical author with 17 books to her credit
One Simple Wish—A woman with a past discovers that dreams really do come true.

Join us for an exciting journey West with
UNTAMED
Available in July, wherever Harlequin books are sold.

MAV93

Take 4 bestselling love stories FREE

Plus get a FREE surprise gift!

Special Limited-time Offer

Mail to Harlequin Reader Service®

3010 Walden Avenue
P.O. Box 1867
Buffalo, N.Y. 14269-1867

YES! Please send me 4 free Harlequin Temptation® novels and my free surprise gift. Then send me 4 brand-new novels every month, which I will receive before they appear in bookstores. Bill me at the low price of $2.44 each plus 25¢ delivery and applicable sales tax, if any.* That's the complete price and—compared to the cover prices of $2.99 each—quite a bargain! I understand that accepting the books and gift places me under no obligation ever to buy any books. I can always return a shipment and cancel at any time. Even if I never buy another book from Harlequin, the 4 free books and the surprise gift are mine to keep forever.

142 BPA AJHR

Name	(PLEASE PRINT)	
Address	Apt. No.	
City	State	Zip

This offer is limited to one order per household and not valid to present Harlequin Temptation® subscribers. *Terms and prices are subject to change without notice. Sales tax applicable in N.Y.

UTEMP-93R

©1990 Harlequin Enterprises Limited

Fifty red-blooded, white-hot, true-blue hunks from every State in the Union!

Beginning in May, look for MEN MADE IN AMERICA! Written by some of our most popular authors, these stories feature fifty of the strongest, sexiest men, each from a different state in the union!

Two titles available every other month at your favorite retail outlet.

In July, look for:

CALL IT DESTINY by Jayne Ann Krentz (Arizona)
ANOTHER KIND OF LOVE by Mary Lynn Baxter (Arkansas)

In September, look for:

DECEPTIONS by Annette Broadrick (California)
STORMWALKER by Dallas Schulze (Colorado)

You won't be able to resist MEN MADE IN AMERICA!

**Relive the romance...
Harlequin and Silhouette
are proud to present**

A program of collections of three complete novels by the most requested authors with the most requested themes. Be sure to look for one volume each month with three complete novels by top name authors.

In June: **NINE MONTHS** Penny Jordan
Stella Cameron
Janice Kaiser

Three women pregnant and alone. But a lot can happen in nine months!

In July: **DADDY'S HOME** Kristin James
Naomi Horton
Mary Lynn Baxter

Daddy's Home... and his presence is long overdue!

In August: **FORGOTTEN PAST** Barbara Kaye
Pamela Browning
Nancy Martin

Do you dare to create a future if you've forgotten the past?

Available at your favorite retail outlet.

HARLEQUIN®   *Silhouette*

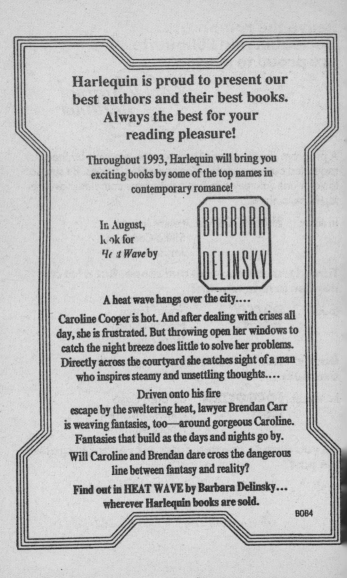